SHE IS THE WIDOW MAKER

SHE IS THE WIDOW MAKER

THE UNBELIEVABLE MR. BROWNSTONE BOOK FIVE

MICHAEL ANDERLE

DISRUPTIVE IMAGINATION

She Is The Widow Maker (this book) is a work of fiction.

All of the characters, organizations, and events portrayed in this novel are either products of the author's imagination or are used fictitiously. Sometimes both.

Copyright © 2018 Michael Anderle
Cover by Andrew Dobell, www.creativeedgestudios.co.uk
Cover copyright © LMBPN Publishing

LMBPN Publishing supports the right to free expression and the value of copyright. The purpose of copyright is to encourage writers and artists to produce the creative works that enrich our culture.

The distribution of this book without permission is a theft of the author's intellectual property. If you would like permission to use material from the book (other than for review purposes), please contact support@lmbpn.com. Thank you for your support of the author's rights.

LMBPN Publishing
PMB 196, 2540 South Maryland Pkwy
Las Vegas, NV 89109

First US edition, June 2018
Version 1.01, July 2018

The Oriceran Universe (and what happens within / characters / situations / worlds) are Copyright (c) 2017-18 by Martha Carr and LMBPN Publishing.

SHE IS THE WIDOW MAKER TEAM

Special Thanks
to Mike Ross
for BBQ Consulting
Jessie Rae's BBQ - Las Vegas, NV

Thanks to our Beta Reader
Natalie Roberts

Thanks to the JIT Readers

John Ashmore
Kelly O'Donnell
James Caplan
Peter Manis
Micky Cocker
Paul Westman

If I've missed anyone, please let me know!

Editor
Lynne Stiegler

To Family, Friends and Those Who Love to Read. May We All Enjoy Grace to Live the Life We Are Called.

1

The five Drow sat around a massive blue-crystal table. They glanced on occasion at a door and waited for the consulate staffer to return.

"Are we sure the new Princess of the Shadow Forged is even in this wretched hive of humans?" Laena asked. The Drow woman didn't want to spend more time on Earth than necessary. "Just because her mother died near this city doesn't mean the girl is still around."

A Drow man frowned. "It's our only real option unless we wish to involve the human authorities or ask for additional help. Our attempts to track her have failed. Someone is using powerful magic to shield her location."

Laena hissed. "The less the humans know the better, and we are Drow. We don't go begging gnomes, Light Elves, or anyone else for assistance. Besides, if more learn of her wish, it'll only cause more trouble for us. It's disgraceful that we can't go and just seize the girl directly."

"We have to be careful about this. Everything we've learned suggests the girl grew up thinking she was human, not even knowing about her Drow heritage. If we approach her too aggressively it might become a problem."

"She'll adapt. The longer we wait, the more of a problem it'll become. At least before she had a Drow parent around her, now she's with this…James Brownstone, another human." Laena sneered. "If he knows about the wish, he'll try to persuade her to use it for him rather than the benefit of the Drow. She belongs with us, and we should do what is necessary to reclaim her."

"But the humans—"

Laena slammed her fist on the table. "I don't care what the humans think. They are barbarians who murder each other with impunity. They lack honor, vision, and strength. We *will* save our princess from them, even if we have to annoy a few people who overly value stability and false peace."

The gathered Drow nodded their agreement.

Someone knocked on the door, and the Drow fell silent. A Light Elf in a suit entered a moment later with an apologetic smile on his face.

Laena resisted the urge to snort. Many Oricerans were adapting to human ways, and so many of them were obsessed with precious human technology. Turning Oriceran into Earth wasn't the answer. They needed to understand that.

Oriceran might have problems, but it'd accomplished things the humans couldn't even dream: a peace that had lasted centuries, and stability—a balance within their world.

Such concerns would have to wait. The princess needed to be retrieved. Laena could worry about the future after they accomplished that.

"I'm sorry for the wait," the Light Elf apologized. "After speaking with my superiors, I've been authorized to pass along some information, including some warnings that you should be aware of so you don't cause trouble for yourself or the local Oriceran population. We've established good relations here, with not too much resentment."

"I heard a Light Elf was murdered by a human earlier this year, and the human authorities let the murderer go because he claimed he had been cursed. That seems like a lot of resentment to me."

The elf's face tightened. "There are difficulties when different populations mix. It's...to be expected."

"I know how *we* have handled that."

The Light Elf narrowed his eyes. "So do I, which is why I don't want you causing trouble for the rest of us. But some of this is about protecting you from trouble as well."

Laena didn't care about inconveniencing anyone. She didn't even want to be on Earth. If the previous princess hadn't run off, they wouldn't have had to come sniffing for her daughter.

She glared at him. "We're Drow. We're more than capable of protecting ourselves from humans."

The Light Elf sighed. "Normally I'd agree, but when it comes to James Brownstone..."

James shifted in the comfortable seats of his F-350. His

phone was to his ear. "Yeah. Shay is out of town on another acquisition trip."

Alison sighed on her end. "She's *always* out of the country."

"Goes with the job, kid. Can't expect artifacts to be hidden underneath some Walmart in Madison, Wisconsin."

"I guess. Do you at least know when she'll be back?"

James chuckled. "She'll be back when she's back. She's not great about giving me her schedule, but it should be soon. She told me it'd be a short trip when she left."

"Well, maybe next time we can make it a family trip. Stevie mentioned a family trip to Europe they were taking during summer break; actually for the whole summer break. Maybe we can do something like that, Dad."

He'd still not gotten used to being called Dad, but at the same time his heart warmed every time he heard it. With Alison, Shay, and his new friends in his life and the Harriken threat destroyed, for the first time in a long time James had allowed hope to sneak into his heart.

"I don't know." James sighed. "That might be too long for either Shay or me to not go on jobs."

"It doesn't have to be for the whole summer. Maybe you can do some on the side. There are plenty of bad guys in foreign countries. I mean, you can do what you did in Japan."

"It wasn't exactly a sightseeing trip, though, and other than some good *yakiniku* places, I wouldn't want you hanging out at a lot of the places where I had to go."

Alison groaned. "Just saying we can be like Stevie's family and go see some place other than Los Angeles. I've lived there all my life until now, and I don't get away from the school in Virginia all that much."

"I've lived in LA all my life, too."

"Then you know it's boring."

"It's a lot of things, but I would never say it's boring." The warmth of familial discussion faded as fatherly paranoia grew. "Wait. Stevie? Who the he...who is this guy, anyway? I don't remember you mentioning him before."

"Stevie? Stevie's not a guy. Stevie's a girl. She's in a couple of classes with me. We aren't that close, but I talk with her sometimes."

James sighed in relief. "Oh, good. Just a girl."

Alison laughed. "Seriously? Are you going to freak out about every guy who talks to me? Half this school is guys, you know."

"Not...*every* guy," he grumbled.

The girl continued laughing.

"Okay, come on, stop laughing! So I'm a little protective, okay? That's what fathers are supposed to be."

Alison regained control. "Dad, I can handle a few guys, and it doesn't matter anyway. Everyone knows about the famous James Brownstone, so most of them tiptoe around me anyway."

"Good." James grunted. "Saves me trips and ammo."

The sound of scratching and shifting filled the line. "What?" Alison's voice sounded distant as if the phone weren't next to her mouth. "Really? Okay, just let me finish up with my dad."

"It's okay," James told her. "Do what you need to do."

"Okay, talk to you later. Love you, Dad."

"I love you too, Alison."

James ended the call and glanced out the truck's window at the modest ranch house. The well-maintained yard spoke of care compared to the overgrown messes in front of many nearby houses, but the peeling blue paint revealed issues with time or money.

He looked up at movement in his rearview mirror. Eight men with skull tattoos on their faces were coming up the street. Demon Generals. They were far outside their territory. A bunch of gangbangers gathering conveniently near the leader of another gang didn't strike James as a coincidence.

Really, fuckers? Now I'm never gonna have a chance to talk with Trey.

James stared at the house for a moment. Trey's grandmother had lived in that house for longer than either Trey or James had lived. He'd come there to catch up with his friend, but didn't want to interrupt Trey's time with his grandmother or risk the wrath of the cane-wielding old woman inside.

Too bad. He'd managed to make it a few days without kicking anyone's ass.

He texted Trey.

You might hear some noise in the next few minutes. Stay inside with your grandma.

Shit. You sure?

Just some DG pussies looking to cause some trouble. They should have stuck to their territory. Besides, I owe these guys for trying to screw with my stuff.

You do what you do best, Big Man.

James slid his phone back into his pocket and stepped out of his truck onto the sidewalk. The Demon Generals continued to saunter in his direction, half on the sidewalk and half on the road. He waited until they were about ten yards out.

Time to make an offer. If they chose to reject it, that was their own damned fault.

"Go home." The bounty hunter punctuated his sentence by cracking his knuckles and glaring.

The gang members all laughed.

"Who the fuck are *you*, you ugly piece of shit?" one of them called. "Your mama drop you in a vat of wax or some shit when you were born?"

James assumed the man was a leader or lieutenant, given that he was a yard ahead of any of the others.

"Doesn't matter who I am. This neighborhood doesn't need any trouble, let alone the old lady in the house you're heading to. You're outside your territory, too."

The gang member grinned; he had murder in his eyes. "That bitch Trey's in there. You think you some sort of friend of Trey's? You can't trust that bitch. He's not even playing the right way. That fucker worked with the cops to get some of our homies locked up, so now we're gonna have a little talk with that squealing little bitch and his grandma, too. If you don't want to get fucked up, get the fuck out of here. You understand me, you ugly sonofabitch?"

James heaved a sigh and ran a hand over his close-cropped hair. "I don't give one shit about whatever gangland bullshit rules you think exist. From what *I* heard, you were going to steal from a man, and a concerned neighborhood citizen made sure that didn't happen."

"Yeah, bitch. We heard that big-ass bounty hunter James Brownstone was out of town and shit, so we was gonna show him he ain't all that."

James grunted. His reputation was spreading over the world, but many people still managed not to know who he was. The combination might prove useful in the future, but for now he wanted to use it to screw with the gang member.

"Hey, what's Brownstone look like? I'm curious. I heard he's been on television a lot."

"I don't watch TV. That shit rots your brain."

The gang members all laughed.

"And Brownstone?" the gang member continued. "Ugly motherfucker, I've heard. Got all these tattoos and funny shit on his face." The man's eyes widened. "Shit, bitch." The DG sneered. "You're even uglier than I heard. Guess I should watch more fucking news so I can identify all the ugly motherfuckers around LA."

James gave the man a feral grin. "You assholes were trying to steal from me, and Trey made sure that didn't happen. Now I'm gonna repay the favor. You can turn around right now and walk away, or I can beat the living fuck out of you to teach you a lesson about respecting personal property."

"Fuck you, bitch. I heard that when a bunch of hitmen came, you ran off to hide behind a bunch of Marines like a pussy. You ain't shit. I bet you got a bunch of people to help you with them Japanese fucks, too. You're all smoke, no fire, Brownstone."

His men hooted and hollered behind him.

James snorted. He'd only led the hitmen to Camp Pendleton to avoid collateral damage. The stubborn refusal of some in the underworld to see the obvious amazed him at times. If the Demon Generals didn't want to believe his reputation he'd make them feel it in their broken bones and battered faces, and then they could pass it along to other assholes who didn't believe it.

Even without his amulet, James could take eight pieces of shit without pulling his gun.

Some of their humor drained from their faces, as if they could sense his violent intent. The gang members spread out and widened their stances.

He'd give them credit for being a little aware, but only some.

"You assholes probably aren't worth any real bounty money even all together." James shifted to his side. Their leader might talk a lot of shit, but he wasn't one of the bigger guys. "Still gonna take you down."

"Bring it then, bi—"

The bounty hunter rushed forward and slammed a fist into the largest gang member. There was a sickening crunch and the man flew backward several yards. Half the remaining men stood there stunned.

Three of the others, including the one who'd been speaking, charged James. The leader got an elbow in the face for his trouble. He collapsed to the ground, blood spewing from his destroyed nose, but James' restraint saved the man from death.

The bounty hunter grabbed the next two men by the

necks and slammed them together. They went down in a tangle of limbs and groaned.

Another gang member managed to yank his gun out with a trembling hand and fire. His shot didn't come close, and James' fist landed square in the man's face. He collapsed and his gun skittered across the ground.

James spun and bowled into another gang member. The thug's outstretched arm braced his fall, but the crack and the scream that followed proved he'd broken it.

That gang member's pain was only beginning. A powerful kick launched the man into his two remaining friends, who were both pointing guns. They grunted and fell back and no shots ensued.

James was done with the farce. He yanked out his .45 and pointed it at the men.

"Drop your fucking guns or I will give you new nostrils."

The remaining Demon Generals dropped their guns and raised their hands. Most moaned in pain. Their blood stained the pavement, but all remained conscious.

"You got two choices, fuckers." James gestured with his gun. "I could just cap you now. It might cause me trouble, but I'm really fucking annoyed that the assholes in your gang thought they could steal my shit, and even more fucking annoyed that you came to mess with Trey over it at his grandmother's house."

The wounded gang members only groaned in response.

James leaned forward. "My old house got blown up, if you hadn't fucking heard, but I'm guessing you did because your boys came to rob me. Point is, I lost a lot of stuff, so I value what I have. But I'm feeling generous, and I'm trying to be more peaceful, if only to give my parish priest less heartburn. So get your asses up. I'm gonna call the cops, and they are gonna arrest your asses and drive you to jail." He glared. "Or we can go for Round Two and you can see who is still alive at the end."

Fear, not arrogance, ruled their faces now.

"Fuck, Brownstone. We'll go. *We'll go*. Just don't kill us. We surrender and all that shit."

"If I hear about you coming near Trey or his grandmother again I will fucking end you. You understand me?"

"Yeah, bi...yeah, we understand, sir."

James shook his head.

Fuck, I can't go anywhere without trouble following me. I bet Shay doesn't have to deal with this shit.

The Light Elf sighed after he finished his briefing for the Drow. "And that is just what this Brownstone did to the Harriken for killing his dog and threatening his family." He shook his head. "If you're right and this half-Drow girl he is protecting is in fact a princess, I would recommend avoiding any blunt options such as kidnapping."

Laena narrowed her eyes. "We didn't say anything about kidnapping her."

The Light Elf shrugged. "There are no humans here. We don't have to maintain a false front about Oriceran unity. You're Drow. I know all too well that many of your solutions lack elegance."

The Drow's mouth curled up in a sinister smile. "Do you now, Light Elf?"

"Yes. So think of something better. Maybe negotiate? Don't go looking for trouble with this man—you might not be able to deal with it, and you'll exacerbate local tensions."

Laena snorted. "So be it. We have time. We only care that she's safe. But we will be watching. Don't worry about your precious local relationships."

The Light Elf gave her a polite nod. "Thank you for your understanding." He headed back out the door.

The Drow rose, nodding to a woman across the table. "You'll handle this. Find him, please him, free him, or kill him. I don't care what method you use, but we're not going to wait around because everyone's afraid of some human who can use a few artifacts. Be cautious and minimize the attention you draw, though. We want to avoid trouble with the local authorities, human or Oriceran. It'll only make it harder to find the princess."

The other Drow smiled, then her body shimmered for a moment and her appearance changed. The thin, athletic body of the ebony-skinned and white-haired Drow was replaced by a luscious and voluptuous pale blonde in a low-cut red dress.

"Don't worry," the disguised Drow assured Laena. "It's been some time since I've had a chance to test my skills. This will be most enjoyable."

Laena nodded, wondering if she'd made a mistake. Removing the Widowmaker's leash might cause some diplomatic trouble down the line, but such a price would be a trifle if they could recover the new Princess of the Shadow Forged and her wish.

A few minutes later, the Light Elf watched from down the hallway as four Drow and a blonde woman stepped out of the consulate's foyer. He was insulted that they hadn't pretended to care for at least a few more minutes.

He shook his head. "Drow never listen."

2

James nodded as he took in his almost completed house. A few issues with the plumbing and electrical contractors had slowed things, but the new two-story home would be ready for Alison's return.

"Yeah, this will do. She'll like it."

Trey cleared his throat from behind the bounty hunter. "My nana wanted to go outside and beat those motherfuckers down, you know. She was all bitchin' about them fools makin' noise and how this used to be a nice neighborhood and that."

James grunted. "Sorry. I didn't pull my gun right away, so I hoped *they* wouldn't. I was wrong." He shrugged. "Dumbasses got what was coming to them."

"Nah, it's all good. You had my back. Shit, you had Nana's back too, and the whole neighborhood's. She ain't mad at you. She's mad at those fools for causin' a ruckus."

"You had my back when I was out of the country, Trey. You stopped those guys, and for that matter, it's amazing how many upgraded supplies mysteriously appeared on the construction site." James grinned. "I'm gonna do both of us a favor and not ask where they came from."

Trey shrugged. "All that magic and shit, you know. Maybe it's some Keebler Elves doing it, you know what I'm sayin'? And fuck the Demon Generals. They are bitches anyway, even in their *own* territory. I remember hearin' about them losing a bunch of guys in an alley a while back. Nobody knows what the fuck happened to this day. They just be yowlin' to make people think they badass, you ask me."

"Father McCartney would say something about living by the sword, dying by the sword."

Trey laughed. "That's why you bring a gun, motherfucker. Ain't you ever seen *Raiders of the Lost Ark?*"

James chuckled, remembering a few other times where the gang leader had mentioned a classic movie. His grandmother was ninety-two. Maybe *she* was the reason.

Trey's phone rang and the gang leader pulled it out. "Shit. I gotta take this. Give me a sec." He stepped toward his truck, the F-350 he'd purchased after admiring James' for so long.

The bounty hunter was never going to complain about someone appreciating a quality classic vehicle.

With his friend on the phone, James figured it'd be as good a time as any to catch up on his emails. He started searching through the queue for anything of interest.

DO YOU WANT TO COOK OUT-OF-THIS-WORLD-BARBEQUE LIKE NADINA? BUY YOUR TICKET NOW!

James selected the email. A photogenic picture of the first Elf winner of *Barbeque Wars: The Next Generation* greeted him along with her "Oriceran Fusion Barbeque Tour" schedule. He saved the message for later and continued searching.

The heavy level of barbeque-related spam always made checking his mail an adventure. He should unsubscribe to at least half of the site feeds and mailing lists, but he didn't want to take the chance he might miss out on important barbeque-related news.

He spotted a message from the lawyer handling Alison's adoption and opened it.

"Damn."

James had hoped to have the adoption wrapped up as quickly as possible, but residual legal issues, including confusion about her mother's whereabouts and some concerns over the man adopting her being the same man who killed her father.

The lawyer didn't have huge worries, but James had hoped to have everything ready at the start of summer break and it might take longer than that. It shouldn't be a huge deal as long as it still happened during the summer.

James sighed and continued checking his messages. One from Sergeant Mack caught his eye.

The police wanted him to bring in a level-one bounty. The bounty might roll on someone else important in local organized crime.

James stared at the email with a frown. He wanted to help his friend and temporary landlord, but he didn't have time to go after every low-level piece of shit in a city like Los Angeles.

"A bunch of dumbass knucklehead fucking morons," Trey mumbled as he stepped back toward James. "If I wasn't around they wouldn't be able to find their own asses." He shook his head. "Sorry about that."

James glanced between Trey and his phone several times. "Gang shit?"

"Yeah, gang shit. But, you know, you've got to get up and make the motherfucking donuts every day to get paid, right? So fuck them bitches."

"What if you had another option to make money?"

"Huh? What other option? I ain't much for standing there with a smile while some fucker spits in my face because I forgot his extra fucking ketchup. I'd punch his ass out."

James shook his head. "I had something else in my mind, though it might still involve punching people."

"Like what?"

"You work for me."

Trey stared at James with disbelief plastered all over his face. "Doing what? Guarding your shit full-time?"

"No. You're street-smart, and you understand when to get rough and when not to." James shrugged. "Look, you know me and you know my rep. I'm a class-six bounty hunter. Normally I don't even get out of bed if we're talking under level three, sometimes even level four. I try to keep my life simple." He let out a long breath. "And I try to keep on good terms with the cops, even if a lot of them don't like me."

"Fuck the 5-0."

"Nah, most of them are good."

"Yeah, maybe. That Sergeant Mack is all right. I'll admit that."

"They're asking me for more and more favors, shit like tracking down lower-level bounties."

Trey rubbed his chin. "And you need some like motherfucking sidekicks to go in there and take down bitches who can't set themselves on fire or raise the dead and shit like that? Just normal motherfuckers?"

"Exactly."

The gang leader glanced around for a moment as if to confirm no one else was listening. He leaned in and spoke in a low voice.

"Yeah, I'm interested, Mr. Brownstone," Trey replied, his voice different in tone, rhythm, and inflection. "My Nana has never been happy with me running a gang. Blames herself for me being a criminal. She wants me to live clean…or at least clean*er*, you know?"

James chuckled at the sudden change in speech pattern. Maybe Trey wanted to convince him that he could function in different social environments.

It was working. If anything, the man already demonstrated he could modulate himself better than James could.

"Being a bounty hunter is still a rough job," James cautioned, "but I don't take down people who don't have it coming. You'll be helping get scum off the street."

"Hell, I guess you're a bad influence." Trey's gaze flicked to his truck. "Maybe a good influence. I don't know. But, yeah, I'm down with it." His face lit up. "Can I wear a suit? I look badass in a suit, but I don't ever have a reason to wear one with my boys."

"I don't, but sure. Knock yourself out." He furrowed his brow. "I'm gonna have to do some paperwork, set up something. I guess we can call it 'the Brownstone Agency.'"

He nodded, satisfied with the name. "And I think we should incorporate the gang somehow. Just need to think about how to best do that."

"Huh?"

"Look, I get it. The gang's about protection and being in control, but I'm saying I can provide good-paying work, maybe in shit like information collection, so none of your boys are doing anything that might get the cops on them. And as far as the neighborhood being protected, I still fucking live here, so my reputation will help keep it safe. Every time someone like the Demon Generals show up and cause trouble *I'll* handle it, and that means fewer people will come. Hell, they were the first ones in a while to try something."

Trey nodded, a thoughtful expression on his face. "If you say so, Mr. Brownstone. I'll have to talk with my boys and see what they think."

"It's okay. I'm still figuring out the details."

James shifted his attention from Trey to the house. He wasn't sure if starting a bounty hunting agency and involving a number of gang members would fall under his KISS philosophy of life in the short-term, but was confident that in the long run everyone would be better off—including the neighborhood and the cops.

One man—even one man with a strange alien amulet—couldn't keep a city like Los Angeles under control.

Is that what this is about? Shay has me mostly convinced I'm some kind of alien, so I want to dig my little tentacles deeper into the city to prove I'm human?

James grunted. He didn't fucking know about that, but he knew he liked the sound of the Brownstone Agency.

Tyler smiled to himself as he finished pouring a mojito and set it in front of a tired-looking older man at the bar. He surveyed the room, which was filled with customers, here for both the drinks and the information. He almost wanted to laugh at how things had changed in such a short time.

Not that many months ago he'd have been lucky to have a dozen customers at any given time. He made decent money as an information broker, but the stench of failure had hung over the cracked and worn furniture and walls of the Black Sun.

Now everything had been remodeled, including his attitude. There were often a few cops in the bar, unofficially enforcing the place's status as a neutral ground. People felt comfortable drinking there, which meant he made more money, and once they got a few drinks in them, they might even buy some information.

Tyler's smile faded and his hands clenched into fists. His success had come at a price; a big price. He'd helped make James Brownstone a lot of money. The fucking smug bounty hunter'd had the balls to place bets on his own life.

A good businessman never passes up an opportunity for profit, so Tyler hadn't, but that didn't wash out the lingering distaste over helping Brownstone profit.

Fuck you, Brownstone. I've got everything I need now, plus the cops helping me out. I know AET hates your ass, and someday you're going to die and I'll still have the Black Sun.

"Everything all right, Tyler?" asked an attractive brunette on the other end of the bar; his new assistant, Kathy.

"It's fine. Just thinking over some shi—"

The din of conversation in the bar hushed as everyone looked toward the front door. Only the blare of the game from the television kept silence at bay.

A mouth-watering blonde in a tight red dress sauntered through the door with a coy smile. Her heels were so high they were probably illegal under some obscure California law.

Tyler swallowed. The woman was easily the most beautiful ever to set foot in the Black Sun.

The crowd parted before her. Whispers restarted, followed by normal conversation. The blonde hopped atop a bar stool, placed one pale hand over the other, and beamed a seductive smile at Tyler.

"W-what can I get you?" the man managed to get out.

The blonde leaned in, giving him a nice view of her ample cleavage. "I'm less interested in a drink than a little information." She winked.

Tyler tore his gaze from her breasts to stare into her crystal-blue eyes. "Information? I know a lot of things. I think you'd find what I can do with some of that information...surprising."

A soft laugh escaped her lips. "Oh, I'm sure I would be. I know I've come to the right place." She reached over and placed a soft hand on his. "And I'm sure you can help me."

"What sort of information were you looking for?" Tyler managed to inject some suspicion into his voice despite the distracting body in front of him. He was supposed to be a damned professional, after all.

"Oh, it's nothing serious, I can assure you. It's just, I was looking for a man and he doesn't seem to be at his old place. I'm not from around here, so I don't know where to look."

"I know a lot of people. Maybe I could point you to someone who knows this guy."

"Excellent. His name is James Brownstone."

Damn you, Brownstone!

Tyler slowly pulled his hand back and kept a fake smile on his face despite the rage threatening to make him combust. That asshole bounty hunter now had this super-model-quality woman looking for him. Annoying. No, not just annoying. *Unfair.*

"Brownstone, huh?" the bartender mused. "Yeah, I can tell you *exactly* where to find him right now. I'll even do it for free. Consider it a service for a beautiful woman." He grinned.

The blonde clapped her hands and kept them together. "Wonderful. Where is he?"

"Last I heard, he's at some sort of meeting with the cops in Laguna Beach. He's supposed to be there for a couple of days. Don't know much else. It was kind of a rumor thing to begin with."

"I see. Thank you for your information." The blonde rose, gave Tyler a final smile, and made her way to the exit.

Kathy finished pouring a beer for a man down the bar and walked toward Tyler. "Laguna Beach? Why did you tell her Brownstone's in Laguna Beach, let alone having some sort of special meeting with the cops? I haven't heard anything about that. I don't remember the last time I heard about Brownstone going to Laguna Beach."

"I'm doing her a favor by steering her away from that

asshole. I'm hoping she'll get frustrated enough to stop looking for Brownstone."

Kathy snorted and turned away.

Tyler ignored her. She was smart enough to probably see through his excuse, but plausible deniability could get a man far in the world. It sure had helped him.

Two AET cops stepped inside and eyed the place. No one paid them any heed as they headed to the bar.

One of the cops stopped and glanced at a man in the corner. "Hey, Jackson!"

A huge man with a shaved head looked up from his beer. "What?"

"Don't let me see you on the outside, man. We will have to grab your ass."

The huge man stood. "Give our fine boys in blue two drinks on me, Kathy."

The assistant bartender nodded and smiled and the cops faced her as she poured their drinks.

"I figure," the cop began, "it'll take at least ten minutes for us to finish these."

Tyler nodded. "Thanks for keeping it neutral, gentlemen."

3

James stepped into the bank. A long line of bored-looking customers snaked toward the single open teller while four empty stations mocked them. A couple of bankers sat behind their desks on the other side of the room, tapping away at computers.

Glad I don't have to wait in that line.

He glanced up at a clock. He was a few minutes early for his appointment, and he wasn't familiar with the protocol for this sort of meeting. Waiting seemed pointless when the person he was there to meet didn't have any customers or even look that busy.

The banker might be in the middle of some furious document review, but with only ten minutes until the appointment that was doubtful.

James made his way to the personal bankers' desks on the opposite side of the room, stopping in front of a desk behind which sat a blond pretty-boy a good ten years younger than him. The nameplate on the desk read Douglas Nestor.

The banker looked up at him with a blinding smile. A person almost needed magic to get teeth that white.

This is the guy I talked to on the phone? He looks like a douchebag.

Doug nodded toward the customers in line for the teller. "I'm sorry, sir. If you want to cash a check, you'll need to get in the teller line. I don't handle that sort of thing. You can also go down the street to the 7-11. They'll charge a small fee."

James grunted. "We have an appointment."

The banker looked James up and down with obvious disdain. "I specialize in business accounts, so I'm pretty sure you have an appointment with someone else, Mister…"

So you are *a douchebag, don't only look like one.*

"Brownstone. James Brownstone. We spoke on the phone earlier about the agency I'm starting."

Doug stared at the bounty hunter as if he were having difficulty processing the revelation.

"Oh, I'm sorry, Mr. Brownstone." Doug smiled and motioned to a chair in front of his desk. "You aren't what I was expecting."

The chair creaked as James sat. "You were expecting a bounty hunter to wear a suit and tie?"

Well, Trey wants to wear one. Guess that's not crazy.

"No, no, it's not that. You're a man of some means, at least based on the assets you have at this bank. I didn't expect you to be so…" He gestured toward James. "Well, um…interesting? Maybe I was expecting some sort of uniform or something, like Grayson. I saw an interview with their commander the other day. Interesting group."

James narrowed his eyes. "Grayson's boys aren't bounty hunters, they're mercenaries. Not the same thing at all."

"Oh, yeah, right. Right."

"I'm a successful bounty hunter. High-level bounties pay a lot of money, and I've invested well. I have no idea what other bounty hunters look like, only myself. Is that gonna be a problem?"

"No problem, Mr. Brownstone." Doug's forced smile returned. "Like I said, you weren't what I expected. I apologize for any offense." The smile didn't reach his eyes.

He picked up some papers and straightened them before setting them aside. "From what we discussed earlier, you're not interested in a small-business loan?"

"No, I don't need one. I have plenty of money to fund everything myself."

"Are you sure, Mr. Brownstone? You see, a lot of people like to operate businesses out of their home, but from what you said earlier, you're going to have employees. An office space can do a lot to make you seem more professional and help your reputation."

James was surprised. After everything that had gone down during his raid on the local Harriken headquarters and some of the ensuing media coverage, he assumed most people had some clue who he was. The Demon Generals not recognizing him on sight was one thing, but they at least knew of his dealings with the Harriken.

Doug being a douche earlier and comparing him to Grayson he'd attributed to the man not liking bounty hunters, rather than being clueless. James didn't worry too much. It didn't matter if the douchebags didn't understand, as long as the scumbags did.

"You don't watch a lot of tv, do you, Doug?"

"No, not really. Why?"

"My reputation isn't much of an issue. People know that I can get the job done, and soon they'll understand that my employees can, too. We don't need an office for now, but I'll keep what you said in mind."

About the *last* thing he wanted to do was help Doug earn any commissions.

The banker nodded and disappointment settled over his face. "We'll just get your business accounts set up for you then." He pulled his keyboard over and tapped away. "You sure you're not interested in a business equipment loan? Drones and computers can be expensive, and I'm sure you use all sorts of fancy and expensive tools when you're going after your man, and all that."

James grunted. Doug the Douche was right, but that didn't change the fact the bounty hunter didn't need any loans.

"Nah. I'm good. Just the business accounts. Just need somewhere to park money and pay expenses, and some accounts to pay employees."

"And you're already bonded and insured?"

"Yeah. You can't get your license without being bonded and insured."

Doug nodded. "I was going to recommend a company otherwise. I can get you competitive rates if you're interested."

Just give it up already, Dougie-boy.

James shook his head. The question reminded him of

something important. He'd have to call his insurance company, in addition to getting licenses for his new employees if they wanted to collect on the actual bounties. Just another thing to add to his ever-growing bullshit list of tasks for starting up his agency.

Yeah, this is gonna suck way more than I realized.

The lawyer pushed a huge stack of papers across his desk toward James.

"Mr. Brownstone, these are your copies, and I've also emailed them to you. The paperwork finalizes the creation of your S Corp, but I'm somewhat concerned about your rather tenuous grasp on some of the employment regulations, based on our earlier conversation."

James shrugged. "Not like I've employed people before. If I knew it all I wouldn't need you."

The lawyer chuckled. "I suppose that's true, but keep in mind that a lot of different agencies have their interests in these things, both in terms of taxes and employee treatment. You need to cross your I's and dot your T's. I'd love to have your future business, but I also try to make sure my clients don't step into unnecessary trouble."

James sighed. So much for keeping it simple. He'd figured starting the Brownstone Agency wouldn't be a huge deal—that he'd just pay for a business license online and have a lawyer draw up a few employment contracts—but between visits to the bank, the police department, city hall, and the lawyer, he'd burned off a few days accomplishing not much of anything other than paying people for the privilege of condescending to him.

James groaned. "That's what I'm paying *you* for, right? To let me know what I need to do?"

"I can help you with contracts and that sort of thing, but I'm more concerned about your compliance with employment and tax law on a continual basis, especially given that you seem to want to bring on a lot of questionable employees." The lawyer rolled his eyes.

James didn't give a shit what the man thought about his hiring practices. Bringing on gang members would take them away from a criminal career. It was a win for everyone including the cops, even *before* considering that the men were going to help bring in other criminals.

"Who knew it'd be so fucking hard to start a business?" the bounty hunter muttered. "No wonder I never wanted to be an employer! The government is doing everything it fucking can to make it a pain in the ass."

The lawyer chuckled. "That's California for you."

"Well, what should I do if you *can't* help me with that sort of thing? I don't have time to go to law school right now."

"It's easy. I'll send you the contact information for several reputable HR management firms. You can outsource most of the busywork to them. You just have to pay them and sign things on occasion then."

James grunted. "So they'll be able to handle all the damned regulations and taxes and shit?"

"Yes, that's a good summary of what they'll accomplish. Given your unique needs, I'll narrow the list down to those who have some experience in dealing with the interface of magic and employment law."

"Thanks." James glanced at a clock on the wall. "We almost done? Not trying to be rude, but I have my third appointment at the bank today to continue setting up all the freaking agency accounts. I swear they're just making me come back so they can try and push more products on me."

"Probably." The lawyer shook his head. "You've signed everything I needed you to sign. I'll let you know if anything comes up."

I'm sure the Department of Screw Jobs will show up soon and demand some additional money.

James was halfway to the bank when his phone announced a call from Shay.

"Hey," he answered, the built-up irritation from the last few days obvious in his voice.

"Hey, Brownstone," Shay replied. "What are you doing, dumbass? You sound kind of pissed."

"I've been running around town the last few days trying to get a business set up. It's been fucking annoying, and there's this douchebag at the bank I want to throw across the room because he doesn't know how to take a hint."

"Huh? Business? What the hell are you talking about? You decide you don't want to be a bounty hunter anymore? Gonna open a flower shop? Sell candy?" Shay gasped. "Fuck, you're gonna open up a barbeque place, aren't you?"

"No." James chuckled and slowed to a stop as a light turned red. "I've decided to start the Brownstone Agency. I'm gonna hire a few guys like Trey and use them to go after low-level bounties so I can concentrate on big fish. It'll also help with bullshit like the cops asking me to track down some pissant bounty they need for whatever reasons."

"Huh."

"Huh? What do you mean by that?"

"I mean that's smart," Shay clarified. "Not sure I can keep calling you a dumbass. Having help isn't such a bad thing. Even *I* have Peyton."

The light turned green and James pulled forward. "Even if it's smart, I'm sure I'll make a mistake sometime."

Shay laughed. "Yeah, probably. You do like to charge in and solve your problems by ass-kicking. Works great most of the time, not so great when you're dealing with normal people."

"Yeah, don't I know it." James grunted. "So what's up? I don't even know where you are right now."

"Australia. What, you want me to call you every night and tell you I'm okay?"

That didn't sound half-bad, but he wasn't about to say that to Shay.

Shay snickered. "I'm heading to the Outback as part of a job. Not sure how well even my satellite phone will work where I'm going, so I'll be out of touch for a few days."

That didn't sit well with James. It didn't matter that Shay had proven she could kick ass and then some. Recent events had pounded home how weird and strange the world could be, even by his already generous standards. His encounter with the despair bug in Japan had reinforced how strength and weapons might not matter if something could get into your head with magic.

James wanted to tell her it was too risky, but he had no damned right to tell an ex-killer and current tomb raider to avoid danger—especially considering the kind of bullshit *he* pulled.

"You don't show up within five days I'm coming to find you."

"I'm a big girl, Brownstone. I don't need someone to come looking for me."

"You're not a big girl. You're a tiny woman."

"Yeah, compared to *your* Neanderthal ass, sure." He swore he could hear her rolling her eyes over the phone.

"Look," James began, "I'm just saying… You've had my back more than a few times. Not such a big deal if I have yours."

Shay snorted. "That's because you're not as careful as me. I don't need you to have my back."

"You telling me you could have handled the *Brujos Rojos* yourself on our first job together?"

"You're damned right I could have. Probably could have killed them quicker than you."

James laughed. "You thought you'd be able to shoot them."

"I just wanted to let you feel like you were doing something useful."

The bounty hunter chuckled as he made a right turn. "I need to feel useful?"

"Yeah, you do. Otherwise, you get all mopey and obsess over barbeque."

"Nothing wrong with barbeque. It's better than pizza."

"Hey," Shay retorted, venom in her voice. "There's no reason to start talking crazy."

"Just saying," James mumbled.

"Anyway, I'll be fine. If someone kills me, I'm confident you'll come and burn down their entire city, so it works either way. Don't worry me about me. This job is more tedious than dangerous."

James pulled off the street into the bank's parking lot. "I've got to go. Bank meeting."

"Look at you, Mr. Business Jerk! So many meetings."

"Call me when you can. Alison's worried."

Shay sighed. "Okay, I will. Talk to you soon."

The call ended, and James finished parking, then stepped out of his truck and shook his head.

Shay might be fighting strange warlocks or monsters in the Australian Outback, but James had been facing the deadliest of foes for the last few days: bankers, bureaucrats, and lawyers.

4

Widowmaker reclined on the soft leather sofa, watching the 108-inch television that dominated the wall. Humans were pathetic in many ways, but she'd grant they did leisure well.

The bed in the rental home was so soft it felt like lying on air. The spacious windows allowed plenty of light in during the day and a beautiful view of the city at night.

She could quibble, but it wasn't a bad place to spend a few weeks while she hunted down James Brownstone and the princess.

The Drow smiled, thinking about how easy everything had been so far. Even if she'd not immediately been able to find the man and her info from the Black Sun had been useless, the mission wasn't a burden.

Securing a temporary base had been her greatest concern, but it'd turned out to be trivial. Taking a home from an unworthy man had been her initial plan, but Laena's orders had implied Widowmaker wasn't supposed to make too much public trouble—not that she refrain from killing anyone.

Indeed, there was no way her superior would have given Widowmaker the task if she'd been worried about deaths other than James Brownstone's. All magic had a price, after all, and she was more than happy to pay for hers with the lives of the unworthy.

But the precious technology of the humans had made slaying an unworthy man for his home unnecessary. The Drow assassin had been able to rent a beautiful and palatial rental home in the Hollywood Hills with the help of an app on a phone.

Widowmaker clucked her tongue and returned her attention to the television. "Fools invite strangers into their homes."

On the screen, a husband and wife pair of assassins attempted to slay each other in an orgy of firearms and fisticuffs. The on-screen guide informed her the movie was *Mr. and Mrs. Smith* and had been made over thirty years prior. The Drow found it enjoyable, as far as human trash went, though she found the killers weak compared to her.

As far as she could tell, unlike some other human movies she'd seen, the assassins' only real power was their mastery of human weapons, especially firearms. They wouldn't last ten seconds against a Drow.

Something else appealed to her on the screen, and it was as good as time as any to change her appearance. The more confusion she sowed, the more difficult it'd be for the authorities to track her activities.

Widowmaker rose from the couch, took a deep breath, and reached into her blood. Warmth passed over her as her form shimmered and changed to that of the brown-haired woman in the movie. Her garment became a high-slit black dress.

She checked the on-screen guide again.

"Angelina Jolie, hrmm? Good name for a killer." She tilted her head, realizing it was the name of the actress and not the character, but that didn't change her opinion.

Widowmaker sashayed over to a full-length mirror and stared at the image. She tsked and slightly shrank her lips.

"Every man wants a dangerous woman, right?" Widowmaker snickered. "I should use this."

She inhaled deeply. Time to harvest and improve Earth…one man at a time.

The Drow sauntered from her *borrowed* Ferrari toward the entrance of the dance club. The bouncer grinned at her as she headed in. His eyes were hidden behind his sunglasses, but he had likely focused on her body considering her current appearance.

The thumping bass shook Widowmaker's bones as she slipped through the crowd. Humans did *so* adore their excesses. She didn't understand how they could appreciate music that seemed more concerned with vibrating their bodies than reaching their ears.

So many aspects of human culture lacked elegance. She was aware of some of the diversity that existed on Earth, but the lowest common denominator seemed to dominate all human cultures.

Laena was right. Humans were barbarians. Sometimes interesting, but always inferior.

A man in a tight sparkly shirt smiled at her. His hand lacked a ring, but she didn't even return the smile, which deflated him. She needed someone unworthy, not just any horny man.

The Drow continued deeper onto the dance floor, the flashing strobe light highlighting the moving bodies. A few glowing orbs pulsed overhead; pathetic creatures of Oriceran more concerned with mere energy than culture.

This is what Earth would bring to Oriceran. Decadence. Decay. Barbarism. We need to get the princess away from these creatures.

A group of red-faced men in business suits in the corner caught her attention. They danced by themselves, and poorly at that.

Widowmaker stopped to watch them. The men all appeared middle-aged. She had a better chance of finding a married and desperate man among the group. For that matter, he didn't even need to be that desperate, given her current appearance.

She inhaled, enjoying the mingling scents of sweat, perfumes, and colognes. The hunt always relaxed her.

A few of the businessmen leaned toward some nearby women and spoke to them. The Drow couldn't make out what they were saying over the music, but the women recoiled after a moment and hurried away.

One of the men flipped them off. The rest of them spoke among themselves for a few seconds before heading to a nearby table off the dance floor.

Pathetic, but maybe even more useful.

Widowmaker grinned and moved forward, shaking her hips and moving with the music as she passed through the crowd and closed on the lone businessman. The wounded male ego was always the easiest to manipulate. It didn't matter what species the male was.

A glint of gold on his finger caught her attention. A married man. That meant her little jaunt wouldn't be a waste of time. Others might find her methods brutal, but her limited choice of targets spoke to her restraint; an elegant choice that reinforced the importance of honor.

All he has to do is honor his vows. He'll make his own choice. It'll be his own fault.

The Drow closed on the dancing man. His eyes widened and he smiled as she ground against him. They moved together to the beat.

The businessman slipped his arms around her waist and leaned close to her ear. "Did anyone ever tell you that you look like a young Angelina Jolie?"

Widowmaker forced a giggle. She doubted he could detect the insincerity, given the stink of alcohol hovering around him.

"Thanks. You're pretty good-looking yourself." The Drow did a little spin. "What's your name?"

"I'm Charles, but everyone calls me Chuck."

"Angie," she lied.

"Seriously?"

Widowmaker nibbled her lip and shrugged. "Funny how things work out."

Chuck laughed. "Yeah."

I have him.

"I come here all the time," she said. "I haven't seen you here before."

The easiest way to get a man to do exactly what you wanted was to put him on the defensive. Men, human or otherwise, were simple creatures, desperate to prove themselves.

"I'm not from LA. I'm here for a conference, just here for a few days." Chuck raised his eyebrows in a pathetic attempt at being seductive. "A man could make lots of memories in a few days."

"I can imagine."

The song changed, the new one overwhelming any attempt at conversation. As they continued to dance, the man's body responded to her efforts. A couple of minutes later he leaned close to her ear again during the extended finale.

"I'd like to take you back to your place, rip off that dress, and fuck you until you scream," Chuck suggested. "Maybe that's too forward or just the tequila talking, but it's also the truth."

The song ended, and Widowmaker smiled and licked her lips. "I'd kill to try that." She stepped away and winked over her shoulder. "I'll be waiting out front. If you want, you can even drive my Ferrari. I've been waiting for a man who can handle both of us."

Chuck's wide grin split his face, and he rushed toward the table with his friends. He slipped his wedding ring into his pocket and tossed a few bills on the table. "Don't wait for me. I'll get back to the motel...later." He winked.

A few of his buddies high-fived him as Widowmaker disappeared into the crowd. It'd be good for him to struggle to find her for a few moments. The tension and uncertainty would increase his desperation.

I can't wait to show you my little trick, Chuck.

A few minutes later, Widowmaker pulled the Ferrari up to the sidewalk and smiled at the waiting man. She caught sight of the last few seconds of a worried expression before it changed into a happy one.

The Drow batted her eyelashes. "Wasn't sure if you'd be willing to leave your friends, so I headed out." She shrugged. "A little test."

"You're a dream come true, Angie. Fuck my friends."

"I'd prefer if you fuck me, Chuck."

They shared a laugh. Widowmaker slid to the passenger's seat and patted the driver's seat.

"I've never driven one of these." Chuck got in.

"And I'm willing to bet you've never been with a woman like me, not that I mind. I can tell that you're special, Chuck. You're going to please me tonight in a way you've never pleased a woman."

"You're damned right I will." The businessman closed the door. "Guess it's just my lucky day all around."

"Let's make sure to exchange numbers afterward. I know you said you're only in town for a few days, but maybe we can see each other when you swing through town again."

"Oh, Angie, I'll exchange numbers after I exchange some fluids."

As Widowmaker stared down at the naked Chuck on the bed, tranquility and warmth spread through her. The man stared at the ceiling with a huge smile on his face and his eyes didn't move. The laceration across his throat was a second smile.

I hope you had fun before the end, Chuck.

A dark mist surrounded the Drow's outstretched hand. The man's blood flowed from the wound into a large nearby cup, and she licked her lips as she thought about the power contained in the precious life fluid.

Life was wasted on people like Chuck, but she'd do her best to turn that wasted life into something worthwhile.

"Rejoice, Chuck. You will help me find the Princess of the Shadow Forged. Your meaningless existence has been transformed into an important tool for the Drow."

The Drow lowered her hand to the man's throat. The wound sealed itself, but it was far too late for the man. She hadn't even bothered to note when his last breath left him.

Widowmaker picked up the cup of blood and gulped down the warm, metallic contents, savoring the flavor. Even as the liquid slid down her throat, she could feel the power of the sacrifice flowing through and warming her.

Something about drinking her victims' blood satisfied her more than just leeching soul energy directly. Maybe if she were a royal it'd be different, but she would have a hard time finding a substitute that came with the satisfaction of the first drop as it hit her tongue.

"Thank you again for your sacrifice," Widowmaker

whispered, wiping blood from her mouth. "And I'm sure your wife will appreciate being free of scum like you."

The Drow woman sighed and raised both hands in front of her. Dark, shadowy rings circled her hands as she chanted in Drow. More rings appeared in the next few seconds until they ran up the entire length of both of her arms. She finished her chanting and thrust her arms over the body.

The rings shot toward the man and spread until he was surrounded by a blanket of darkness. A few seconds later, the shadow and the body winked out of existence. No one would find him, and soon her appearance wouldn't even be the same.

Widowmaker chuckled. "Let's see the humans find him in the World in Between."

Lieutenant Maria Hall stifled a yawn as she clicked around on her computer. Too many damned criminals had kept the AET officer busy, and the looming threat of budget cuts kept her neck and shoulders in a permanent state of tension.

She couldn't believe they would even *consider* a cut to the AET budget. It was downright insane, given the shit that had happened in recent months. If anything, they should have been talking about doubling or tripling their budget.

Fucking asshole pencil pushers. They'd probably be happy with nothing but stupid bounty hunters running around dealing with shit because they can get the corporations to kick into the bounty pool.

She gritted her teeth. Cops should be the ones handling criminals, not scum like Brownstone who were all but criminals themselves.

Hell, the guy was *worse* than a criminal. He caused mass destruction, and half the city acted like they wanted to blow him for it. The larger his reputation grew, the more people like him would crawl out from under the twisted rocks they were hiding under, and soon the city would be nothing but a battleground for magical freaks.

You don't win a war by nuking yourselves, idiots.

Maria let out a long sigh and picked up a Styrofoam cup of coffee. A few sips of the hot brew helped calm her down.

She clicked on her To be done folder. AET might not be dedicated to investigation, but that didn't mean she couldn't poke around during her free time.

A file caught her attention. She clicked on it and her frown deepened.

A fuzzy image of a woman taken at long range from a drone dominated the top half of the file. Links to various notes and emails covered the bottom.

"Oh yeah, almost forgot you. You're Brownstone's little female friend."

The lieutenant's previous attempts to track down the woman had ended in failure, but she refused to believe the woman couldn't be identified. Sometimes finding a criminal was a simple matter of looking in the right place.

Maria leaned back and took a deep breath. It was time to hit up a few of her old FBI and Interpol contacts.

5

James returned to his plate for another attack on the delicious brisket. The sauce at Low and Slow in LA was no Jessie Rae's God Sauce, but the nice Kansas-City blend on the brisket satisfied his tongue and stomach.

He eyed the trays covering the table with beef and pork ribs, brisket, and pork steaks, with three different sauces: Kansas City, St. Louis, and their version of sweet and spicy Oriceran fusion.

Every Oriceran fusion sauce he'd encountered lately was the same thing: someone's take on Nadina's show-winning efforts. The elf's influence was definitely spreading, but the cost of the Oriceran herbs and spices made it a pricey experience for a dedicated barbeque lover.

James wondered if that was half the point. It wasn't like he'd priced all the ingredients in Nadina's sauces. It'd been easy to make a profit off curious people.

Trey and Sergeant Mack sat across from him. Both men

launched vicious assaults on the tray of ribs in front of them.

The police sergeant glanced at Trey and James. "I've talked it over with my captain and he's a bit skeptical given Trey's past, but because the Brownstone name is attached and you've even got a company set up, he's more than willing to have us start funneling lower-class bounties to your agency." Mack held up a rib and shook it as he spoke. "But the captain made it clear that if shit gets fucked up all bets are off, and this doesn't say we're gonna lay off the gang. If they do something illegal they will be brought in." He frowned at Trey. "Don't think because you're working for Brownstone that any of us will look the other way."

"Don't worry, Mr. 5-0. I know all that shit, and all *you* need to know is that I'll catch all the bounties you need as a duly authorized representative of Mr. James Motherfucking Brownstone. If any of my boys are stupid enough to get caught by you, they deserve what they get."

The bounty hunter chuckled and picked up a glass of beer. He marveled at Trey. The gang leader could switch up his language in an instant to whatever people expected. It was a good strategy, because it made people underestimate his intelligence. Hell, even James had.

So many criminals focused on puffing up their abilities when the opposite could be a useful strategy.

"None of these low-level bounties are going to be dead or alive," Mack noted. "I want that damned clear. We're not turning LA into some sort of warzone."

Trey shrugged. "I ain't no killer anyway. I've only stepped up to protect me and mine. I just want to make the streets safer for my nana and make a shit-ton of money."

"Fair enough."

James nodded in approval of Trey's answer. He'd expected pushback from the police. From their perspective, it might look like his new agency was taking control of a street gang for its own uses.

I kind of am. Huh.

The cop nodded and focused on James. "You thought much about expansion?"

James groaned. "I've gone through more paperwork the last few days than I have in the last ten years. I've got some stuff set up to potentially bring on other people from Trey's gang, but I'll have to figure out jobs for them other than just being my eyes and ears."

"I'll be honest with you, Sergeant," Trey interjected. The gang leader shook his head. "Some my boys don't know much shit. Hell, they can't *spell* 'shit.' Not all, but some."

"Big surprise," the cop muttered.

Trey chuckled. "Glass houses and all that stuff. I've seen plenty of your brothers in blue who are stupider and more thuggy than a lot of my boys."

"Yeah, can't say you're wrong there." Mack furrowed his brow. "I've got an idea, Brownstone, and if you're already done the paperwork to at least get them on a payroll or something it'll be easy. They don't even have to learn any new skills."

James finished a rib before responding, "What's the idea?"

"Property insurance jobs."

Trey laughed. "You mean you think my boys can go over and inspect people's property and shit? Hell, I like 'em, and even *I* don't think that. There's giving people a chance, and then there's just being stupid."

James shrugged. "He's got a point."

The cop shook his head. "No, you're not following me. What I'm saying is that just having a few of these guys around will scare off people, especially now that people are associating them with you. I'm talking about them just kind of being symbols; living warnings." He leaned in and lowered his voice. "I think your little stunt with the Demon Generals has slowed their expansion plans. The gang task force is grumbling a little, but also pretty grateful. Those bastards have been getting nastier despite losing a lot of guys." He nodded Trey's way. "And they're calling his boys 'the gang that doesn't bang.'"

Trey snorted. "Whatever. It's like the Mafia after prohibition. Nothing wrong with going legit after you've proven you're badasses."

Mack held up his hands in front of him. "Not saying we're complaining. Just saying a known quantity can help."

Trey looked at James. "I say stick the boys in suits. That can be our Brownstone Agency trademark. We'll be the best-looking sonsabitches in LA."

"*You* can wear suits." James grunted. "But *I* don't wear suits."

"Shit, motherfucker, you're the boss. You do what you want. I'm just saying it's easy for my boys to sit around in suits, but they can knock some heads if necessary."

Sergeant Mack sighed. "We don't want this to be some sort of turf thing. The point is de-escalation, not more trouble."

Trey shrugged. "We can call the cops, even. See, we're all law-abiding and shit. That's the whole point."

James thought the idea over. He'd wanted to utilize the gang more and was already depending on his reputation to keep his neighborhood in check, so it wasn't like this was something he'd never thought of. But the more people who got involved, the more complicated his life would become.

Fuck. Not like I can do anything about that. The Harriken made sure of that, and I'm adopting a half-Oriceran teenager and guarding a wish for her. Kind of hard to keep shit anywhere near as simple as I wanted.

Guess that's why parents are always bitching.

James took a long draw of his beer. "It's a good idea. I'll talk to the HR company to see if we'll need any more bullshit paperwork."

"I've got another idea." Sergeant Mack averted his gaze. "I'm guessing you won't like it, but hear me out."

The bounty hunter set his beer down. No one pitched an idea with "hear me out" unless they knew the next few words were utter bullshit.

"What now?" James asked suspiciously.

"Look, your reputation is big. National-news big. I've known you for years, and I know how well you've been doing the job, but all this Harriken shit, both here and in Japan, took it to the next level."

James shrugged. "Yeah, so? The asshole at the bank didn't know who I was. Not so famous."

Trey chuckled.

Sergeant Mack shook his head. "Criminals know, and that's what matters. We can start leveraging that now that you're going to have an agency and employees." He pointed at Trey. "He's right. We get his guys visible in uniforms or suits or whatever, then we get you out there doing…you know, PR. Commercials, interviews, that sort of thing; really spread the word. People see somebody they associate with James Brownstone, they'll think twice about causing trouble."

James stared at the cop like he'd lost his fucking mind. "I'm not some celebrity. I don't do that kind of shit. I kick ass, and I get paid for it."

"But you also have a reputation as the man who beat a group of hitmen; the man who took out the Harriken, not just here, but in their home base."

"The Japanese police haven't officially said I did that," James muttered.

Trey and Mack snorted in unison.

"I've seen crap on the internet." The cop pointed to Brownstone. "Fan sites. Surprised people aren't trying to email you."

"They probably are. Not like I publicly post that shit."

"Once you get your agency going, maybe you should. You can leverage those fans to spread the word," Mack suggested.

James narrowed his eyes. "I don't really like where this is going."

"Look, we both know you're about a lot more than just money. We can use your employees to amplify your reach, and that means a lot of lower-level crap stops just because people are afraid. You can use it to your advantage. The higher-level guys who aren't afraid will think you've gone soft, maybe you're easier to take out."

Trey looked over his shoulder like he expected King

Pyro to be there. "Like to see them bitches go after James motherfucking Brownstone and see what they get. More fuel for the rumor mill is what I'm saying will happen. Either way, it works."

James polished off the last of his beer as he thought over the explanation. Like everything lately it seemed overly complicated, but he figured the cop would know better than him how to deal with crime in a more systematic way.

"Okay, I guess I can see how that much would be useful, as long as we balance it right. I don't want everyone underestimating me, just the top bastards. If I'm gonna fucking embarrass myself, I want it to be helpful."

He deliberated for a few seconds to decide whether to go for more brisket, ribs, or a pork steak. He decided to first hit the former and follow up with the latter.

Sergeant Mack nodded toward Trey. "He can bring in a lot of the low-level bounties to establish the reach of your agency, then you can hype it a bit. Hell, I'm sure I can get some departmental PR resources dedicated to this."

"I'm willing to do it, but are you sure it's a good plan?" James asked. "A lot of people in the department don't like me. That shit they did at the Black Sun is weird."

"Yeah, heard about that, but it's got its advantages, too. Besides, we cops care more about stopping crime than who gets the credit. Yeah, not going to lie, more than a few people have it out for you—especially AET—but that doesn't change the fact that if we can get a city-wide reduction in crime off your reputation alone, it doesn't matter what they think."

"Okay. Just give me some time to let it sink in."

The three men fell into silence as they continued their exploration of the intricacies of meat and sauce.

About an hour later, meat filled James' stomach. Too full and bloated, but he'd gladly pay the price for the experience of eating all the delicious meat.

James flagged down a waitress, then spotted a barbeque cookbook on a stand near the wall in the back. He stood and walked toward it.

"What's up?" Trey asked.

"Nothing, just something personal."

"Badass Barbeque with Tom," James read.

The owner walked from behind the counter. "It's by my uncle, God rest his soul. We brought it over for a bit of color."

"I used to have a signed copy."

"What happened to it?"

"It got burned up in a fire," James rumbled.

Some sonofabitch blew up his house and took down his signed cookbook collection with it. Shay's use of a hidden library warehouse made a lot of sense in retrospect.

The owner glanced between the book and Brownstone several times. "Look, we don't get a lot of celebrities in here."

James grunted. "I'm not a celebrity." His gaze cut to Sergeant Mack.

"You were on TV several times." The owner shrugged. "And we know how much you love barbeque. I'm willing to trade you the book, which is signed by my uncle. In exchange, you sign ten of our t-shirts."

"Hell, yes!"

The owner grinned. "I'm glad we could do business, Mr. Brownstone."

"You could have bargained his ass higher," Trey called from the table.

James was almost back to his apartment when his phone chimed with a text from Trey.

Those motherfuckers from the BBQ place are already selling those signed shirts online for a grand a pop. Eight are already sold. You should have bargained his ass higher.

The bounty hunter chuckled.

Dumbasses. I'm not a celebrity.

Whatever you say, motherfucker.

6

Maria's desk phone rang. It was too damned early for the phone to be ringing. She hadn't finished her second cup of coffee. Or her third, for that matter.

Freaking Weber. He was slacking off.

"Lieutenant Hall, LAPD AET."

"This is Special Agent Danforth from the NYC FBI Field Office."

Maria's heart kicked up. "You have something on my mystery airport chick, don't you? Please tell me you're about to make my day. It's been a real shitty week."

"We got a request to run the image through some additional facial recognition programs and databases we have, and we got a tenuous match. And I mean *very* tenuous. This shit wouldn't hold up in a court in some banana republic, let alone get you a warrant or before a grand jury."

Maria scoffed. "I'll worry about getting that far later. Just give me what you've got. This is important."

Agent Danforth sighed. "You're not going to like this, Lieutenant."

"I don't like a lot of shit, but I'm AET and a big girl. I can take it."

"The only match we have is for a dead woman," Agent Danforth explained.

"'A *dead* woman?'" Maria echoed.

"The picture vaguely matches a hitman we were tracking in the general New York City area for a while. She ended up being killed by another hitman. They burned her house to try and cover up the crime."

Maria rubbed the bridge of her nose. She hadn't expected tracking the woman down to be easy, but she hadn't expected a dead woman to show up either. "And you're sure she's dead? She was positively identified a hundred percent?"

"Yeah, dead. We recovered DNA from the body. According to our DNA records her name was Lisa Sellers, but we're pretty sure that's not her real name—and there's evidence that her birth records were manipulated. Not exactly unusual for some of these high-end killers. Not like they are going around using their real names on the job, and a lot of them have gotten good at covering their tracks with tech or magic."

Maria frowned. "Send me the DNA profile and I'll see if I can collect some samples for matches."

"Lieutenant, this is a wild goose chase. Lisa Sellers is dead. We investigated the scene thoroughly. I'm only calling you because an old buddy of mine put out the call that you needed help, and I just wanted to make sure that if you heard about Sellers you wouldn't waste time chasing a ghost."

"Maybe she is a ghost or a zombie or some shit, but I'm AET. We deal with magic all the time. Maybe some necromancer decided that Sellers or whatever the fuck her real name is needed to rise again. Please just send me that DNA profile, and I'll waste my time if I think I need to. Thanks, though. I needed this break."

"Huh. Good point, and you're welcome. If it *does* end up being Sellers, let me know. You're right. These days we can always say, 'Stranger things have happened.'"

"Will do, and thanks again."

Maria hung up the phone. Her gut told her this *wasn't* a necromancer or some sort of strange Oriceran bullshit.

No, this killer was still alive. She was running around LA helping Brownstone kill people, and Maria would track both their asses down and catch them in the middle of a crime. Even if her department didn't focus on normal killers, she could use resources related to enhanced threats and their associates.

"Working with a hitman now, Brownstone? Why does this not surprise me? I knew you were a piece of a shit, and you're an accomplice to murder." Maria brought up the drone photo from the airport and grinned. "You've got most of the LAPD snowed so I might not be able to get you first, but I'll be able to bring in your floozy killer friend, who is already supposed to be dead, and I'll bet that pisses you off enough that you do something stupid I can finally grab you for." She closed the image. "I hope you enjoy going to an ultramax, Brownstone. I'm sure there's tons of guys there you helped put away."

A notification popped up on Maria's computer. She clicked on it and ground her teeth.

"You've got to be fucking kidding me!"

Officer Malley scribbled a few notes on his pad. The gathered visiting businessmen were pale, but he wasn't sure if that was from fear or hangovers. Several of the men could barely stand. Most rested in chairs on the edges of beds in the motel room.

He didn't frown, even though he didn't like the idea of a bunch of hungover businessmen wasting his time.

"So, do you know the name of the woman your friend left with?"

The most vocal of the group, John, shook his head. "No. He told us not to wait up for him, but he never came back."

"And this was last night?"

"Yeah. Chuck likes to party, but he always comes back, and he's not answering his phone. We think something happened to him. Something bad. Maybe they got carjacked or something."

The cop shrugged. "Look, I don't think it's been enough time for us to do anything. Your friend has barely been gone."

John shot to his feet and swayed for a moment. He gulped as if trying to avoid throwing up.

"My brother is a cop in Dallas," he said, glaring at the cop. "I know you don't have to wait twenty-four hours or anything to report a missing person, so don't feed me that 'enough time' bullshit."

Officer Malley frowned. "Watch yourself, sir. I'm not saying you have to wait twenty-four hours. I'm saying he's a grown man who didn't come back to a motel room after leaving with a beautiful woman, not some kid who disappeared in the mall."

John sighed and sat back down. "I'm just saying this isn't like him."

The cop looked down at his notepad. "You also said, 'a super-hot chick in a super-hot dress. She looked like a movie star, and we didn't get why she'd even want Chuck, and we were all jealous.' You don't think that maybe your buddy decided to say fuck it to the conference and spend a day banging some piece of tail he'll never land again? Especially if his wife isn't around to crowd him?"

"Why wouldn't he answer his phone then?"

Officer Malley laughed. "Are you *shitting* me? Do *you* answer the phone when you're having sex?"

John shrugged. "I guess that makes sense."

"Look, this is LA. I'll tell you what this probably is. Annoying, but not sinister. That chick is probably some aspiring actress or model trying to make ends meet as a waitress. She goes to the club, sees some middle-aged dude and decides she can get a new sugar daddy, but she's got to put her work in first." The cop shrugged. "The best thing you can do for Chuck is convince him not to send her any money once he heads back home."

John nodded. "Yeah, you're probably right. I don't know if I should be pitying him or calling him a lucky bastard."

"Hey, as long as he doesn't give her any money he's still getting to have sex with a hot chick, and his wife will probably never find out." Officer Malley closed his notepad. "If anything else comes up let us know, but I guarantee you that your boy will call you the day of your flight back, panicked and in a rush because he lost track of time between all the sex and blow."

"You really think he's okay?"

"I think he had a better night than any of us."

Kathy finished pouring a beer and pushed it over to a customer. The door opened and a curvy raven-haired woman stepped into the Black Sun. The bartender didn't recognize the woman, but something about her seemed vaguely familiar.

She snickered to herself after a few seconds. It wasn't that the woman was familiar, it was just that she didn't fit in with the rougher crowd.

Kathy was attractive, but this woman could stop traffic. Hell, she could stop air traffic thirty-five thousand feet up. She only seemed familiar because it was the second ultra-hot woman who had come into the Black Sun recently.

The bartender didn't care. Jealousy was for the insecure. Kathy trusted in her combination of brains and beauty.

Yeah, wonder if that blonde is pissed at Tyler. Wonder what her deal was? Just looking for the biggest and toughest guy to fuck?

The dark-haired woman grabbed a stool. "I'll have a Black Russian."

The bartender nodded and grabbed the bottles to prepare the order. "Haven't seen you around here before."

"Oh, I've just heard this place is popular lately."

"Yeah, you could say that." Kathy finished preparing the drink and set it in front of the woman.

The woman took a sip and smiled. "There are a lot of things in human civilization to despise, but this planet is good at booze."

Kathy laughed. "I hope so. Otherwise, I'd be out of a job."

The dark-haired woman offered a weak smile and fell silent as she nursed her drink.

Kathy didn't mind. Some people wanted to talk to bartenders, but a lot of people just wanted to drink a little booze somewhere other than home. Besides, a place like the Black Sun could be entertaining because of the crowd alone.

A good twenty minutes passed as the bartender served refills and a few new customers. The dark-haired woman was on her third Black Russian.

The loud conversation of two slick-haired men in suits at a table caught Kathy's attention. They were local Italian Mafia—a diminished presence in LA now between all the competition supernatural or otherwise, but the local Italians still took pride in their traditions and stubborn resistance.

"You hear about Brownstone and the Demon Generals?" one of the gangsters asked; a man named Lenny.

"What about him?" the other gangster replied.

"I heard he beat six of them to death because they pissed on the grave of his dog."

"Shit, that didn't happen."

"Yeah, because fucking Brownstone is known for his restraint." Lenny snorted. "I'm surprised it was only six."

The dark-haired woman picked up her drink and sauntered over to the table. The timing made her intent obvious.

Yet another Brownstone groupie? Bet she's some rich bitch from Coto who got all wet when she found out Brownstone drove through there.

That blonde probably had been, too. Crap, how many of these skanks are going to come to the Black Sun looking for him?

Kathy's face twitched. She didn't like the idea of random hot women showing up and screwing with customers. The Black Sun was neutral ground, not some place for Brownstone groupies to sniff around.

"Care for some company?" the dark-haired woman asked.

The two gangsters exchanged glances and grinned.

"Sweetheart, you get your ass into a chair," Lenny ordered.

The beautiful woman took a seat with a soft smile on her face and her hand on the man's shoulder.

The trio fell into quiet murmurs that Kathy couldn't make out over the next several minutes. The woman stood, and one of the gangsters followed.

"I think we'll enjoy exchanging something valuable with each other," the woman stated and sashayed toward the door.

The gangster winked at his friend and hurried after her.

Once the pair stepped through the door, several men

grumbled. Kathy bit down the laugh at the pathetic jealousy on display.

"What the fuck?" a scarred man at the bar muttered. "Since when does Lenny get chicks like that?"

"Oh, don't worry about it," Kathy told him. "She's hot for Brownstone. I doubt Lenny will get a reach-around even with his pants on."

7

James leaned back in his chair, enjoying the opening banter on the *Sauce Wars* podcast.

"Forget about Nadina." Francis, one of the hosts scoffed. "Not saying she's not cute and doesn't know her way around some sauces, but she's not the be-all and end-all. If everyone's interested in fusion, screw Oriceran. We've got nine billion people on this planet. Hundreds of countries. Why are we getting all impressed by Oriceran spices and flavor combinations when we've got our own? How many barbeque fans could even identify a Moroccan spice combination if they tasted it?"

Ava, the other host, laughed. "Good point. Many people argue about whether certain regional barbeques styles are true barbeque, but I say, bring it all on. Let's mix it all in. Let's get the Oricerans obsessed with *our* flavors, not the other way around."

The podcast paused as James got a call from Sergeant Mack.

"What's up?" James answered.

"I've got a favor to ask."

James grunted. "I thought we agreed to send Trey after the level-ones. That was the whole point of me setting up the Brownstone Agency."

"This isn't about that, and what I'm asking requires James Brownstone, not Trey Garfield. Like it or not, there aren't a lot of other people like you out there."

Don't I fucking know it. If Shay's right, there may be nobody like me on this planet.

"What do you need?" James asked.

Mack cleared his throat. "So, you're not going to believe this, but I just got a notice from AET requesting your help. As in, you were requested by name."

James laughed. "No shit? Why didn't they just call me directly? Not like the cops don't know my number."

"I think Lieutenant Hall would have a stroke if AET did that, and her superiors aren't fond of you either. To be clear, our *local* AET doesn't need your help, but there's been a request from the Detroit Police Department for the LAPD to facilitate you going to Detroit to help *their* AET. They've got some intel that a level-five bounty might be rolling in and they want a little Brownstone backup."

"And they can't handle it? I handle local shit because I live here, not because I'm the only one who can."

Mack sighed. "We've got decent funding in the LAPD. DPD AET? They've got shit for funding. It's amazing they can even field an AET team there. They are underfunded, underpaid, and understaffed, but I've met a few of the guys. They are good cops, and I don't think they would be reaching out if they didn't respect you."

"I'm not some sort of bounty hunter for rent. I don't want every police department in this country suddenly thinking they just have to dial me up and I'll come running."

Fuck. Talk about complicated shit. Shay's deal is running around and doing things, not mine.

"No one's saying you are or that you have to, Brownstone, but if you're willing to go out of the country for a bounty, going to Michigan shouldn't be a big deal. Take a supersonic flight and you could get there tonight."

James grunted. "Are they gonna pay for that?"

"Actually, yeah, and the bounty would be good money. Plus, think about it. This'll spread your rep, so it'll help the Brownstone Agency. I'll push that angle with them so they know you should get something out of this."

"Fine, I'll fucking do it, but I'm not flying until first thing tomorrow morning."

"I'll call DPD and give them your contact information and tell them you're on your way," Mack offered.

"I don't want this shit to become a habit."

"I'll keep that in mind."

"Okay, talk to you later." James ended the call, closed his eyes, and scrubbed a hand over his face.

He took a deep breath. Next week some Mountie might call him up and ask him to go to Ottawa. Or maybe some cop from France would need his help beating down a dragon in Provence. His reputation had grown beyond his ability to manage it.

Fucking Harriken. Because of you, my life will never be simple again. Glad I killed so many of you fucks.

By the end of all this shit, will I need a Brownstone Army?

Trey adjusted his tie in the mirror. The dark suit looked damned good, and the wrap-around sunglasses only added to the hotness. He resembled a badass spy more than a bounty hunter.

"Damn, I look good." He snapped his fingers. "Brownstone *wishes* he could look this damned good."

His phone rang, ripping him out of his self-appreciation. A glance at the phone indicated it was Sergeant Mack.

"Yeah. What's up, Sergeant?"

The cop muttered something under his breath. "It's time to put you to the test. There's a level one we need brought in."

Trey snorted. "Level one? Maybe I should call my nana and have *her* do it. Maybe stop by a kindergarten first for reinforcements." He laughed. "Seriously, that's all you need?"

"It's a nice test case, and this guy's important. We need him to testify against some serious people. Name is Jack Conners, a con artist and low-level street hustler. Not known to be all that violent, but you never know if cornered rats will bite."

"Not even a gangster? This'll be easier than I thought. I can scare this asshole into coming with me."

"This is serious, Trey, even if the guy's not all that important. If he goes to ground or we lose him it'll hurt some of our investigations. Do I make myself clear?"

Trey could imagine the constipated frown on the cop's face. He rolled his eyes.

"Don't worry, Sergeant Mack. I've got this. I'll go you

one better. I'll have this asshole to you by tonight."

The cop chuckled. "If it were that easy we would have already found him."

"Nah, you wouldn't, because you're cops and you don't know where to look. Even Brownstone doesn't always know where to look. A life on the streets means I know what dumpsters to check when I'm looking for trash."

"If you say so. Just bring him in. If this goes well, we can really ramp up bounties for you."

Trey stared into the mirror with a smile. "Like I said, I've got this."

Trey glanced over his shoulder before following the man into the alley. He retrieved a few bills from his wallet and handed them over.

"There you go, now spill with the info."

The man snatched the cash out of the newbie bounty hunter's hand like a hungry wolf going after a steak. "You can't tell anyone I ratted him out. That'd be bad for my reputation."

Trey almost laughed. The only reputation this asshole had was for turning all his money into dust and spending half the week high.

"The Brownstone Agency maintains the utmost discretion for our sources. And I think you'll find being on the good side of James Brownstone is better for your health than the opposite." He pulled his glasses off to glare at the man.

The other man rattled off an address. "Conners is there

now, but he won't stay there long. He moves every week, from what I've heard."

"Thanks for your assistance." Trey slid his glasses back on. "Now I have an appointment with a con man."

During the fifteen-minute ride to the address, Trey considered his strategy. Pulling his gun would only escalate things, especially if he approached the man spoiling for a fight. The police needed the man alive, which meant anything that raised the chances of a fight would only work against him.

Lying to the man was pointless. Only an idiot tried to con a con artist. Trey wasn't above a little deception, but he'd lived his life being blunt and straight-forward. Being a gang leader was all about projecting honest strength.

Con artists, as far as he was concerned, were cowardly little bitches. Gang members provided protection to those who gave them respect. Con men did nothing but take.

Tricking a person to take their money made the man a leech, and Trey would enjoy taking down the parasite.

He frowned, a hint of doubt creeping in for the first time. Taking down bounties didn't bother him, but his talks with the gang had produced mixed results. Most of his boys seemed happy to work for Brownstone as long as they were paid well, but not everyone was convinced Trey was taking the gang down the right path.

No one was willing to risk open revolt against a man backed by James Brownstone, but Trey couldn't guarantee that no one would stir up trouble.

Guess I'll deal with that shit when it comes up. For now, though, I've got a job to do.

Trey pulled his F-350 to the curb and hopped out, then patted his suit to make sure the gun was there. He didn't want to have a fight, but he wasn't going to let himself get shot like a little bitch either. He double-checked to make sure his handcuffs were in his pocket.

Introduce myself and get the fucker to agree to come. Should be easy money.

Trey might admire James Brownstone to the point where he'd purchased an identical truck, but he had no illusions that his boss operated on a level that he could ever hope to achieve. Trey couldn't do the shit Brownstone did.

Most normal people couldn't. He didn't know if it was magic or some other shit, but Brownstone was worth ten men. A little fronting was one thing, but real arrogance would end with Trey's ass six feet under.

Trey adjusted his tie again and knocked at the front door. Someone moved on the other side of the door, and the curtains to the living room window swished. He listened for the sound of a backdoor opening or closing.

"Don't run, asshole," he muttered. "I don't want to get dirt on my suit."

The front door swung open and a skinny white man with short spiky blond hair eyed Trey. The haircut was new, but everything else matched the picture of his target.

This asshole looks like he should be running a fish taco stand on the beach. He's not gonna be a problem.

"Who the fuck are you?" Conners asked. "I don't need religion, if that's what this is about." He spat in front of Trey.

Be glad you didn't hit my new shoes, asshole.

Trey chuckled and slid off his sunglasses, placing them in his front pocket. "That's not what I hear, Jack. If anything, a few gospel songs might be good for a sinner like you. We're all sinners, really. The trick is to just accept it."

The bounty's eyes narrowed. "How do you know my name?"

"Because you were stupid enough to get yourself a bounty." Trey shrugged. "I'll make this easy. My name is Trey Garfield. I'm with the Brownstone Agency, and I'm here to bring you in."

"'Brownstone Agency?' What the fuck is that?"

Trey shook his head. "Brownstone Agency, as in James Brownstone. He's my boss, but he's too busy to go after low-level pieces of shit like you. That's why I'm here." He shrugged. "Let's make this easy on both of us, Conners. You come along nicely to the police station and no one gets hurt. Let's be real—*you* don't get hurt."

The other man's face twitched and he leaned to the side to look past Trey. "Fuck, that's his truck, isn't it? Only that bastard drives some old piece of shit like that."

Trey stopped himself from throwing a punch. Dissing an F-350 should be punished with a beat-down to end all beat-downs. Brownstone would agree.

The advantage of people mistaking his truck for James', however, wasn't lost on Trey. If anything, it'd already de-escalated the situation. Conners didn't try to run.

Time to bring this shit home.

"It's not Brownstone's truck," Trey admitted. "It's mine."

"What? Every one of you fucks drives an old

truck now?"

"Something like that. So, you gonna come or what? I told the 5-0 that I'd have you tonight."

Conners' gaze flicked to the side for a moment. "If that's not *his* truck, then he's probably not around."

"Don't you listen? I told you how this was gonna work. You aren't worth his time."

"Bullshit. You're just some bitch pretending to work for Brownstone."

Trey squared his shoulders. "You're about to make this very painful for yourself, Conners."

Conners threw a punch, but Trey ducked the blow with ease and pounded a knee into the man's crotch.

The bounty let out a yowl. The newbie bounty hunter followed with a rising uppercut and a kick. Conners collapsed to the ground.

Trey slammed the tip of one of his Oxfords into the man's stomach. "Now why the fuck did you gotta go and do that, you stupid motherfucker?" he shouted, his street language, inflection, and rhythm returning. "You almost messed up my fuckin' suit. I ain't even be paid yet and you gonna go all up and cause me trouble?"

Conners stumbled to his feet, groaning. Trey slammed him into the wall and pinned an arm behind his back.

"I ain't gonna be pissed at you for playin' the game, motherfucker, but you're a dipshit. You got yourself the wrong sort of attention. You should just be happy it ain't my boss here. He would've kicked your ass through a window already for being a dumb shit."

The bounty jabbed at Trey's body with his free elbow. Trey returned the favor with a few kidney punches, then swept one of the man's legs, dropping him to his knees. The bounty hunter slammed Conners' head against the wall a few times.

Maybe it was excessive, but it was still nicer than his boss would have been.

"Bitch, please! You think you're all tough? You don't know shit about real fightin'. Street livin' ain't about your bullshit con jobs. Now stop being a pussy. Even if your ass gets away, all that's gonna happen is Brownstone's gonna come lookin', and then you're gonna get the real beatdown."

Conners stop struggling. His bloodied face left stains on the wall.

"You're not shitting me? You really *are* with Brownstone?"

"Yeah, motherfucker. Guess we need to print up some fucking business cards or some shit." Trey cleared his throat, and when he next spoke his voice had shifted from Gangster Trey to Smooth Trey. "Now, you want me to continue beating your ass down on the off-chance you escape? I'll just call the big man up and tell him what happened."

Conners grunted. "I don't want him coming after my ass."

Trey yanked Conners up and handcuffed him. "Damned right you don't." He glanced down at his suit. "Shit, you got blood all over my suit, motherfucker. You're lucky you didn't break my sunglasses."

"I'm sorry. Don't tell Brownstone."

Trey shoved the man out the door.

I should fucking bill the cops for my dry cleaning.

8

James sat behind a table, looking up at the Detroit PD's AET tactical commander, Lieutenant Walsh. The cop was a barrel-chested rusty-bearded man with a good six inches on the bounty hunter. He looked more like a pirate than a cop. Just needed a parrot.

A half-dozen more AET members were spread around the table.

James drummed his fingers on his leg. He didn't know any of these cops, and half-wondered if the whole call for help was part of a plan by the AET officers in LA who hated him.

I wouldn't put it past some of them. That Lieutenant Hall seems to really want my ass in prison.

"Thank you for coming, Mr. Brownstone," Lieutenant Walsh began. "We've been lucky in Detroit that a lot of the high-end bounties pass us over. Not always bad being fly-over country, I guess."

Several of the other cops chuckled.

James nodded. "Mack wasn't exactly forthcoming with the details, so I don't even know who I'm supposed to be tracking."

"We're sorry about keeping this so hush-hush, but we didn't want to spook the guy. We figured that would give you a better chance of catching him before he causes trouble."

James grunted. "Could have scared him off by mentioning me if you didn't want him around here."

Lieutenant Walsh shook his head. "Then we just send this asshole to another city to hurt innocent people. I don't know about you, but that doesn't sit well with me."

James nodded his agreement. He liked Walsh. The man didn't seem like a glory hound.

"Okay, what's the bounty's deal?"

"His name is Jacob Leesom, and, well, this is where things get complicated."

James groaned. "I hate complicated shit. I've found that punching it hard enough makes it simple."

Several of the cops laughed.

Lieutenant Walsh cracked a smile. "Leesom was a necromancer. *Is* a necromancer."

"Motherfucking zombies," James growled.

The lieutenant shook his head. "Not that kind of necromancer, thank God, but he's nasty in another way. You see, he can switch into new bodies. He can't just hop instantly—it requires some effort and like a day from what we understand, so you don't have to worry about him jumping from body to body—but it means we have no idea what Leesom currently looks like. He could be a man or a woman. Elf or human. Young or old." He shrugged.

"How the fuck do you even know he's here?"

The lieutenant moved over to a lectern and tapped a few commands into a keyboard. A police image of a withered husk of a body popped onto a screen in the front of the room. The cracked and dried corpse looked like it might turn to dust at a touch.

"This body was found in an empty apartment a few days ago after someone started complaining about the smell. We brought in some specialists to do some testing, and their results, both magical and medical, are consistent with previous tests of Leesom's victims. This was probably his previous host or whatever you want to call it."

James twitched, heat flooding his face and his breathing turning ragged. Zombies were a grotesque affront to nature and God's plan, but hijacking another person's body to wear them like a suit? Leesom had found a way to make necromancy even more disgusting.

Congratulations, asshole. I'm gonna really enjoy taking your twisted ass down.

"Anything else I should know?" James rumbled.

"Yeah. Because the bodies aren't technically alive by the time he switches into them, they are hard to kill. Just shooting them in the head or heart won't work. You have to…" The lieutenant paled and averted his eyes. "You have to remove the head from the body."

"Decapitate the fucker. Sure thing." James stared at the corpse on the screen. He'd have no problem ripping the fucker's head off.

"Enhanced strength as well."

James snorted. "Not a problem."

Lieutenant Walsh raised an eyebrow. "Well, that was

why we wanted you, Mr. Brownstone. We figured if you can take out an entire gang, you can help with Leesom."

"Just Leesom? He doesn't have some sort of nickname like 'The Bodysnatcher' or 'Jumper?'"

The cops exchanged glances and shrugged.

Damn. That means he's probably not as arrogant and stupid as half the guys I deal with.

Lieutenant Walsh nodded toward the screen. "This guy's a monster. Anything you can do to help us stop him would be appreciated."

James nodded. "Okay, just send me the information on the apartment. I'm gonna want to go check it out myself."

"Sure. One last thing. Uh, after you, do the deed, you're gonna need to bring us his body."

"So this is dead or alive, with an emphasis on dead?"

"Yeah, but to be clear, we need the body. All parts of it, including the head. We're going to have a magic specialist confirm he's dead. You know, dead-dead. Not just undead."

James chuckled. "Decapitate the fucker, bag 'im, and bring 'im in. Understood, Lieutenant."

It didn't seem like telling them he'd taken the heads of bounties in the past had made them feel any better. Everyone looked really uncomfortable.

If you're not already out of town, Leesom, I'm gonna find you and deliver a real death. Then you can go meet the Devil and tell him I'm gonna kick his ass eventually, too.

A few hours later James sat in a White Castle parking lot in his U-Haul. He originally thought about grabbing a

4Runner but figured it'd be easier to hose out the U-Haul if things got messy.

He tossed a slider in his mouth and chewed.

I'm getting fuckin nowhere fast. Glad Shay's not here to see this shit. It's damn embarrassing.

His inspection of the apartment had turned up nothing. Big fat surprise, considering the cops had already been over it. He had no fucking idea how to proceed.

James lived and worked mostly in LA. Outside of that city, he lacked any real contacts. When he'd taken down out-of-country bounties, other people had provided him the information he needed to track his targets, but the local cops had no clue at all where Leesom might be hiding.

Fuck. You ain't in LA, and you ain't got contacts.

James didn't have any ideas about local information brokers he could pay, threaten, or beg for information. Even a pissant Detroit version of Tyler would have been welcome.

His hand dropped to the amulet resting underneath his shirt. He'd separated it from his body with a piece of metal, unsure if he'd need to use it against Leesom.

After his assault on the Harriken compound in Tokyo he'd become less leery of the strange whispering artifact, which made him even more suspicious when he sat and thought through the implications. After all, how did he know the alien artifact hadn't manipulated his mind?

Guess I'll go a few rounds with Leesom and see if I need it.

It didn't matter. The amulet would be useless if he couldn't find the man.

James frowned and whipped out his phone. He might

not have any contacts in Detroit, but he knew at least one person who might be able to help him.

He dialed and waited.

"Brownstone," answered Peyton in a cheerful voice. "How's Detroit?"

James grunted. "You already know about that?"

"I like to keep an eye on important people. I'm less surprised that way."

The bounty hunter considered asking Peyton if he'd heard from Shay, but she still had four days before his deadline and he didn't want to seem like a pussy.

"I need a favor," James rumbled instead.

Peyton chuckled. "Favors are nice between friends."

"I'm tracking a bounty, a level five by the name of Jacob Leesom. The guy can magically hop bodies, and he's somewhere in Detroit. I was wondering if you could poke around and maybe set me up with some leads. There was an apartment where they found this dead magic-infused body, but the place had been empty for months." James rattled off the address. "Any lead would help."

"Sure, I can do that. I'll just need something in return."

"What?"

"Five thousand dollars."

James snorted. "Really?"

"Yeah. I know how much you're going to make off a level five and it sounds like I'm doing a lot of the hard investigative work, so a little reward isn't out of line. Right?"

"Fine. I'll pay."

Peyton clapped on the other end, which made James wonder if he was using a headset.

"Okay, give me a few hours, and I'll get some leads."

James grunted and ended the call. He scrubbed a hand over his face.

Shit. He'll tell Shay, and I'm never gonna hear the end of it.

You've got to be fucking kidding me. Fucking necromancers. You're really asking for it now.

James pushed into the Eternal Shores Funeral Home. Colorful flowers in vases atop a podium, soft lighting, and light classical music greeted him.

After the briefing, he'd checked into Leesom via his bounty hunter apps and sites. Even if the process killed the victim, no one had said anything about the necromancer being able to hop into already-dead bodies. Maybe it was a coincidence, or maybe the man had a new trick he wanted to try out.

James frowned. Or choice three: Leesom found the ultimate place to dispose of bodies, a place no one would blink at being filled with corpses.

Peyton's digging had turned up some unusual financial activity associated with this funeral home and an account linked to the apartment. The cops hadn't looked closely enough.

Based on what Peyton had explained, James suspected Leesom had been using the place on and off for years under different names. The rental and occupancy patterns were odd and erratic on the surface, but when cross-referenced with Leesom's reported activities in other cities they made sense.

The evidence suggested the body jumper would stir up trouble, leave, and hide in Detroit. He'd just gotten sloppy this time.

Sloppy guys were usually desperate guys. Maybe something had gone wrong. Well, if it hadn't before, it was fucking going to soon.

A dark-suited man with matching hair emerged from the back room, a plastic smile on his face. He moved to the podium.

"Good evening, sir. Welcome to Eternal Shores. We pride ourselves are making your loved one's transition as comfortable as possible. How may I assist you in this time of remembrance?"

The transition to the afterlife didn't require more than a half-decent burial and Last Rites as far as James was concerned, but he wasn't there to pick a fight with the funeral industry. Just Leesom.

The man looked James up and down, probably wondering why James was wearing such a long and thick coat in warm weather. Admitting that he was doing it to cover guns, throwing knives, and a machete might be worth a chuckle, but it'd end with the cops getting called if the man wasn't helping Leesom.

Guess it was time to find out.

"Yeah, I'm gonna make this short and sweet," James began. "I need Jacob Leesom. I don't know what his deal is with this place, but I know he's been in contact with you."

The man furrowed his brow. "I don't remember any customer by that name or any clients by that name. You must be mistaken, sir."

James grunted. "Well, who transferred a hundred thousand dollars to this place yesterday? Give me that name."

The mortician's face twitched. "We have a privacy policy concerning clients and their families."

"Yeah, but harboring a level-five bounty is a pretty big deal, especially a sonofabitch like Jacob Leeson. That guy's a twisted fuck. If you knew what he was into you'd be pretty pissed. Kind of mocks your whole job."

"I can assure you, sir, I have no idea of whom you're speaking."

James stared at the man, looking for a bead of sweat or a twitch of the face that suggested he was lying. The man locked eyes with the bounty hunter, angry defiance on his face.

He might be aiding a mass-murdering body-jumper, or he might just be a pissed-off funeral director not liking being accused of being the said body-jumper.

Fuck. Maybe he honestly doesn't...

The bounty hunter's focused on the man's chest. No rise. No fall. James might not be a doctor, but you didn't need an MD to know that living people usually breathed.

"What's the deal, Leesom? This where you dispose of the bodies normally? Why the fuck did you get so sloppy and leave a body at the apartment?"

The funeral director glared at him. "Sir, I'm going to have to ask you to leave, or I'll be forced to call the police."

James shrugged. "Go ahead. Tell 'em James Brownstone says hi."

The man's eyes widened. "James Brownstone? *The* James Brownstone?"

"Yeah, that's me." The bounty hunter grinned.

So some fucking gangbanger in LA doesn't know who I am, but this asshole halfway across the country does? What's up with that? Maybe that'll make this easier.

The man pointed at James. "You're supposed to be in LA."

"Hey, I go all over. Took a few bounties down in Tokyo recently." James scratched his eyelid. "So, Leesom, you gonna come along quietly, or am I gonna have to get rough?"

"I-I…" The man shook his head and snorted. "Why am I so afraid of you? You're just a man."

"Yeah, that's more like it, asshole. Glad you finally admitted who you are."

The fear and concern vanished from the other man's face. "I wonder what I could do with a body like yours, Brownstone."

"Who knows? Soon you're gonna be fucking dead, so it won't matter."

Leesom barked out a laugh. "Dead? I've been dead for a century."

James frowned. Nothing he'd read said Leesom was that old. The man had been skulking about in the shadows a lot longer than anyone had realized, which was all the more reason to end his ass.

"Yeah, this time I'm gonna make sure it sticks." James pulled back his gray coat, revealing a sheathed machete. "Chop-chop, fuckhead."

Leesom threw the podium toward James and he grunted as it slammed into him. He stumbled as his bounty rushed into the back.

James ignored the pain in his chest and hurried after

the necromancer. He bounded into a dark door-lined hallway.

Leesom sprinted down the hall toward an emergency door in the back and crashed through with a grunt. A shrill alarm sounded just as the bounty hunter passed through.

His target ran toward a nearby metal fence.

James whipped out his .45 and put three rounds into Leesom's back, and the man jerked and stumbled. He didn't go down, but the delay gave James enough time to holster his weapon and close half the distance to his target.

"Stop running, asshole," the bounty hunter shouted. "This is just wasting my fucking time."

He leapt toward Leesom as the man hopped on the fence and both men tumbled to the ground, Leesom landing with a hollow thud.

The necromancer backhanded James, sending him stumbling back with pain radiating over his face.

James rubbed his sore jaw. "Nice hit, fucker." He slammed his foot into the other man and punted him a few yards.

Leesom stood and dusted off his suit. "You might be strong, Brownstone, but you don't understand who you're dealing with. I am eternal. Don't you understand that?"

"You're a fucking parasite who should have died a long time ago." The bounty hunter widened his stance and lowered his right hand. "Like I mentioned earlier, I spent some time in Japan recently. There's something I always wanted to try. Maybe you can help with it, but fair warning —it ends with you in two pieces."

Leesom laughed. "If you beg I'll kill you quickly, you arrogant insect."

James narrowed. "Thought you wanted to use my body?"

"Oh, as long as I start the process before you die it's fine."

The bounty hunter gestured for the killer to come at him. "Bring it, asshole. Let's end this shit."

Leesom charged and James whipped his machete out of its sheath in one fluid motion, swinging toward his attacker. The blade connected with the bounty's neck.

"Oh shi—" Leesom began.

The separation of his head from his body punctuated his sentence. His headless corpse collapsed to the ground, and his head rolled for a few feet.

James glanced between the pieces of the corpse. No blood. Not even coagulated blood. He sheathed the machete.

The bounty hunter laughed. "Thanks for being at a funeral home, asshole. Shit, guess I'll just borrow one of your body bags. It's way better than the trash bags I brought."

9

James frowned as he pulled up to the police station in his U-Haul. Several cameramen and reporters stood in front of the police station, their microphones in the faces of the Detroit AET officers, all of whom were wearing their dress uniforms. Several other cops stood on either side of the AET team.

"What the fuck?" James parked the truck next to the street and rolled down his window.

Lieutenant Walsh hurried to the vehicle. "Sergeant Mack said you wanted a little PR. To be honest, we could use a little too, so we called a few people."

James groaned and ran a hand through his hair. "Yeah, I was talking about maybe some interviews and shit. I got a decapitated necromancer in a body bag in the back. You really want to show them that?"

The cop laughed. "They don't need to see that. All they need to know is that a dangerous magical criminal is off the streets." He nodded toward the reporters.

James grunted and stepped out of the vehicle, following Lieutenant Walsh toward a perky blonde reporter near the steps leading up to the front of the police station.

The woman sprinted toward James, meeting him halfway. It was an impressive feat in her high heels. That the cameraman lugging his gear kept up with her impressed James too.

The reporter raised her microphone and looked into the camera. "This is Cara Lamont, live in front of the Downtown Services Precinct Station of the Detroit Police Department. We've just been informed that the infamous Jacob Leesom, a level-five bounty and necromancer known to hop bodies, has been apprehended by James Brownstone, who recently cleared out every Harriken in Los Angeles at the request of the Los Angeles Police Department."

James chuckled. The LAPD had gotten in on the act late by setting up an organizational bounty. He would have killed the Harriken anyway.

The reporter shoved her microphone in James' face. "Mr. Brownstone, your activities have made you famous, or as some might even claim, infamous. Do you have any comment on people who think you might occasionally go too far?"

"I don't go too far." The bounty hunter shrugged. "I go after bounties. If people don't want me after them, they shouldn't get bounties on their heads. Leesom was a bounty. I brought him in. Simple as that."

"I see. What do you think about the fact that the Detroit AET called in an out-of-state bounty hunter to deal with a local problem?"

Lieutenant Walsh grimaced behind the woman.

James shrugged and moved to stand beside the lieutenant. "I think Detroit PD is putting their lives on the line every day for the people of your city, and Detroit AET isn't given the funding they need to do their damned jobs."

A hungry look appeared on Cara's face. "Are you saying the city council and the mayor are responsible for dangerous criminals like Jacob Leesom thinking they can run free in Detroit?"

"I'm saying you need to give your cops the fucking tools they need." He stared straight at the camera, not giving one solid shit about all his live on-air cursing. "Look, if the politicians won't do right by your cops, the people should. Hell, I'll throw down half my bounty from Leeson as a donation to the Detroit AET to help them out. If everyone in the city gives a little they'll have what they need."

Lieutenant Walsh's mouth dropped open, but he recovered once the reporter rounded on him.

"Lieutenant, your response?"

"Uh, I want to thank Mr. Brownstone for his assistance with the apprehension of Jacob Leesom and his generous donation. I consider him a true friend of Detroit police and police officers everywhere."

"Yeah, tell that to that LAPD AET," James muttered under his breath.

Cara looked into her camera. "There you have it. A six-figure spontaneous donation by James Brownstone to the Detroit AET and a dangerous criminal off the streets. I know that I, for one, will sleep a little better tonight. This is Cara Lamont with Action First News."

"We're clear," her cameraman said.

The woman rubbed her hands together and winked at Brownstone. "Are you interested in any further interviews, Mr. Brownstone? We can do some non-live stuff. It'll help if we can edit some of your more colorful language later."

James grunted. "It's been a long day. I'm really not interested."

The woman offered him a business card, although he didn't see where she pulled it from. "Give me a call if you're ever interested in getting a story on the air in Detroit."

James took the card and shrugged. He wanted PR, but he was more interested in LA than Detroit.

"Come on, Nick," Cara called to her cameraman. "I want to get some quick interviews with some of the other cops."

Lieutenant Walsh leaned over to whisper to James as the reporter scurried off. "You didn't have to do that, Brownstone."

James shrugged. "I felt like it."

"How about you come with the team after we get this mess all cleaned up? I'll buy you a few drinks. It's the least I can do."

"A little beer sounds nice."

James sat in an office waiting for the AET officers to finish processing Leesom's corpse. A call from Sergeant Mack shattered his quiet reflection.

"Hey, Mack," the bounty hunter answered.

"Hey, Brownstone. I didn't want to call you while you

were on the job to distract you, but I was just reading some news online and I see you already solved the Detroit AET's little problem."

James grunted. "Got lucky. The bounty underestimated me, and I brought the right tools for the job."

Mack guffawed. "Shit, if there's one man in this country no one should underestimate, it's you. Anyway, congratulations on that, and thanks for helping out the Detroit PD. Thanks for the donation, too. Might not be my department, but I'm hoping your generosity rubs off on the local politicians and citizens."

"I do what I can."

"Good day for the Brownstone Agency."

"Trey texted me about grabbing Conners yesterday."

"That all?" Mack asked.

"What do you mean?"

"Your boy done good. He nailed two other level-one bounties today."

James grunted. "He isn't a boy. He's a damned man, and I wouldn't have hired him if I didn't think he could do it."

"Yeah." Mack chuckled. "Come on, though. What other white-bread bounty hunter would ever think to go to the hood to search for recruits, let alone hire a gangbanger?"

James sighed. "Fuck if I know. I don't know what other people do, and I don't give a shit. All I know is Trey's always given me respect, so I've shown him the same. Not saying him doing the gang shit is okay, but we both know that a guy like him didn't have a lot of good choices in his life."

Mack fell silent for a few seconds. "Not going to say I think it's okay. I'm a cop, but, yeah, I get it. Hood life is tough, and when the bullets are flying you want someone to have your back. I guess it's a good thing you're giving Trey and his boys an alternative." He laughed. "I don't know if you're getting them to leave gang life or if you're just introducing them to a new gang leader."

"I've always had an odd relationship with Trey. Shit, I believe in him. He's my fucking friend."

James rubbed the back of his neck. All these new friends had snuck up on him since Leeroy's death. It wasn't like he hadn't known Trey for years, but they'd never been that close.

He'd been a loner who didn't give a shit, and now he had a daughter, friends, and Shay, whatever the hell *she* was.

Lover? That didn't seem right, considering they hadn't done anything in bed. Girlfriend? He wasn't some punk teen.

"Your house got blown to pieces," Mack remarked. "Most people would have taken the opportunity to leave a shitty neighborhood like that. I've been processing bounties for you for years, Brownstone. I know how much money you must have. You could live in Coto or the Colony if you wanted, but you're staying in some piece-of-shit neighborhood filled with crime."

James snorted. "I didn't have problems before the Harriken, and now they aren't around anymore to *be* a problem."

"Just saying you really think you can revitalize that neighborhood? That why you rebuilt your house?"

"I'm not trying shit, Mack. I just liked my location. I'm rebuilding, and the neighborhood has my back. If it's shitty, then we'll work together to clean it up." James' hand tightened around the phone. He took a deep breath and loosened his grip. "You remember that shit with the first Harriken bounty on me? Some asshole from Laguna Beach called me, said he was representing HOAs there. Didn't want me driving through because they were worried about damage."

"Huh. Didn't know that."

James snorted. "The fucking point is that maybe the people in my neighborhood are poor and maybe a few of them are criminals, but I know they have my fucking back. If I moved to some neighborhood filled with rich pricks, I know they wouldn't give two fucks about me. Yeah, you remember who your friends are when shit gets real."

"I understand, Brownstone."

"Good. Glad we're on the same page."

Nope, I'm not moving.

James gulped some beer. "The assholes with the nicknames are the worst. They always have to give me a big speech about how tough they are before I pound their fucking smug faces in."

Lieutenant Walsh laughed. "Yeah, you're right, when I think about it. Which has been the worst for you lately?"

"This dick who called himself 'King Pyro.' Talk about a fucking ego."

"Yeah, I read about him. The king is dead, long live the king, I guess." The cop smirked.

Several of the other police officers chuckled and nodded in agreement.

Two burly young men in crew cuts advanced on James and the cops tensed and rose from their seats.

James gestured for them to sit down. If someone wanted a few rounds with him, he'd be more than happy to comply. They'd regret it, and the cops wouldn't have to get involved.

"You're James Brownstone, right?" one of the new arrivals asked.

"Yeah. What about it?"

The man stuck out his hand. "I'm Lance Corporal Nelson, United States Marine Corps." He nodded at the other man. "This is Lance Corporal Larsen."

James gave the Marine a firm handshake. "What can do for you?"

"We wanted to buy you a beer."

The bounty hunter shook his head. "I should buy you guys beers, not the other way."

"Nah, you don't get it, do you?"

"Get what?"

"How much great fucking publicity the entire Corps got out of that shit at Pendleton. Our Gunny won't shut up about it, and our CO says recruitment's up all over the country. The least we can do is buy you a beer."

James chuckled. "Your money."

A couple of hours later it was down to James, Walsh, and the two Marines. The beer and whiskey had flowed freely, and the red faces on everyone but James and their slurred speech proved they were well past drunk and all the way to smashed.

James hadn't skimped on the drinks but was only buzzed, not smashed. For whatever reason, it took a lot of booze to get him drunk. Always had.

Guess maybe it's some of that alien shit. Maybe I should be drinking a bunch of Coca-Cola or something to get wasted.

"Shit, Walsh, you served?" Nelson asked. "Why didn't you say so earlier?"

"Yeah. Army, but a long time ago. I got in trouble all the time, though. I barely managed to get out with my honorable discharge."

Nelson eyed the cop. "What? You get in a lot of fights or something?"

"All the time. Especially with Marines."

"You win?"

"Sometimes. Not often enough."

Everyone laughed.

Walsh shrugged. "Plus I used to piss off my CO during PT by leading the guys in ribald cadences. He kept talking about how I was going to get the unit written up."

James looked up from his beer. "Ribald cadences?"

"Yeah, dirty shit. The kind of shit that gets you in trouble with people who want a more…professional military."

Nelson nodded. "Yeah, we got a female Marine in our unit who likes them. She thinks they're hilarious."

Walsh sipped some more beer before responding, though at this point he was so drunk he swayed when he spoke. "I think my favorite always was 'Monkey from the Coconut Grove.' You know that one?"

"Yeah, that Marine I just told you about taught us." Nelson grinned and nodded to Larsen.

All three men stood and opened their mouths.

"Up jumped the monkey from the coconut grove.
He was a bad motor scooter, you could tell by his clothes.
He wore a four-button diddy with a double-knit stitch.
He was a muff-bucking motherfucking sonofabitch.
He had cast-iron balls and a blue-steel rod.
He could hip-fire Vulcan and thought he was God.
Lined a hundred women up against a wall
And on a two-dollar bet said he could fuck 'em all.
Well, he fucked ninety-eight till his balls turned blue.
Then backed off, jacked off and fucked the other two!
Singing hey, I feel all right now
Hey, really out of sight now."

Everyone else in the bar laughed and clapped.

James rubbed his temples. This shit was worse than the Professor's last Bard of Filth competition. At least the limericks didn't go on as long.

"That shit doesn't even make sense," he blurted before even thinking what he was saying.

Walsh laughed. "What doesn't make sense, Brownstone?"

"How the hell would you fuck a hundred women anyway?"

All three of the men laughed even harder now.

Nelson sat down. "Trying to protect your good-guy cred, Brownstone?"

James grimaced. Good-guy cred. That and the fact that

he was a virgin—about the last thing he wanted to admit to two Marines and a cop.

If sex was great, then it made more sense to spend a lot of time with one woman than fucking a hundred. Shay was still waiting for him to make a move and he hadn't. Maybe she still thought he was gay, even if they were together.

He didn't know. Didn't care. Sex would come when the time was right.

"Just saying," James mumbled.

Nelson waved a hand. "Shit, that one isn't even that bad. You want bad? How about this?"

This time the Marine kept his voice down.

"Whip me, beat me, I need love.
Let me feel that leather glove!
Swing it round and let it crack.
Lay that whip across my back.
Walk spiked heels across my back,
Fishhooks through my scrotum sack.
Whips and chains, now they're a blast.
Let's go, baby. Spank my ass!"

Everyone at the table winced.

James stared at Nelson. "You run around shouting this shit all the time?"

I better never get the Professor in the same room as these guys. All those fucked-up sex songs and limericks will probably a blow a new portal straight to Oriceran.

The Marine laughed. "Nope. We can't even do most of these most of the time. It's like Walsh said—you use those cadences, you get in trouble, at least if a tight-ass hears you. But we have bad-ass ones anyway." He cleared his throat.

"Above the land,
Across the sea,
We're everywhere,
We need to be.
We're brothers of,
A special kind,
A better band,
You'll never find.
Band of brothers,
That's what we are,
Fighting evil,
Near and far.
Band of brothers,
That's what I said,
Baptized by fire,
Scarred by lead.
We're lean and mean,
And fit to fight,
Anywhere,
Day or night.
When bullets fly,
And rockets fall,
We'll stand our ground,
And give our all.
We're on the move,
We're on the march,
We're diggin' ditches,
And breakin' starch.
When you hear,
Our battle cry,
You better move,

And step aside.
Band of brothers,
That's what we said,
Mess with us,
We'll shoot you dead.
Band of brothers,
Trained to kill,
If we don't getcha,
Our sisters will."

James grunted. "Now *that* shit I like."

10

James surveyed the empty living room, rubbing his chin. Empty houses unsettled his stomach. They always made him think of death.

A home was meant for occupation. It was so much more than the walls.

This wasn't a home, not yet. It was just wood, paint, and metal, an artifact with no meaning.

This is my land, and this will be my home again. And Alison's. Shit, maybe Shay's in the future.

James grunted. Maybe not. The woman's tastes ran in a different direction than his, and despite their relationship, she still taunted him about his attention to fine detail.

Being concerned about cleanliness and keeping your living space organized wasn't being anal. It was about keeping things simple. Why couldn't Shay understand that?

At least she's not calling me a dumbass anymore. Maybe we're best if we don't spend too much time together? Or maybe we should spend more time together? Fuck, I don't know.

Bill, the construction foreman, sighed. "Almost finished with the plumbing and electrical work, Mr. Brownstone. Plus, your little surprises need to be completed. The exit to the safe room in the basement is pretty much finished, but we're waiting on a few specialty parts before we can get the floor-hatch from your daughter's room into the basement finished."

James nodded. Everything was coming together easier than he'd dared hope. He was half-convinced someone would show up in the middle of construction and launch another few rockets. Even Trey's gang watching the place wouldn't have been able to prevent that.

"How long do you think it'll take to finish up everything?"

Bill shrugged. "A week, tops."

"Good." James nodded and wandered into the kitchen. He still had a few little touches to handle personally, including access issues for Alison's safety hatch. The girl might be able to feel around for the handle, but in an emergency, seconds mattered.

He'd asked Zoe if she could recommend anyone to help him with his problem, and she'd put him in contact with a runes witch who would inscribe a few runes Alison could perceive without normal human sight.

"This shit is really coming together," James mumbled.

A home with a family. Who would have ever seen that coming?

An hour later, after Bill departed, a familiar F-350 rolled up with Trey at the wheel. Two of his gang rode with him.

James waved to the men and sat on the steps of his new porch. The three men stepped out of the truck and moved toward the bounty hunter, hands in their pockets.

The juxtaposition of Trey in his suit and sunglasses with the low-hanging jeans, white beaters, and bandanas of the other two gang members made James snort.

"Sorry I only dropped you a text, Trey," he started. "I wanted to tell you in person that you did a good job while I was gone. Any other problems I should know about?"

Trey shrugged. "Nah. Not really."

"On to everything in the app?"

"Yeah. It's not hard. The only problem…" Trey frowned. "Nah, it's not important."

James shook his head. "Tell me."

"I'm just annoyed, is all."

"Annoyed?"

"They always *run*. No one just gives up. It ends the same way, so why not just give up?"

James grinned. "Yeah. They'll do that at first, until the reputation of the agency spreads. Then you'll be able to get the small guys to surrender, but you'll start to get bored and *want* them to run."

Trey crossed his arms. "You know, we could corner the market on these small guys if we work hard, Mr. Brownstone."

James stared at Trey. The man's shift in language didn't surprise him in and of itself, but the fact the new bounty hunter was doing it in front of two of his gang members did.

"Why so respectful?" the bounty hunter asked, keeping his tone neutral. "You got the suit on now, so you want to dial it down or some shit?"

Trey shook his head. "You're my boss now, Mr. Brownstone, not just a man in my hood. I respected you before, but now I've also got to set an example for my boys. Respect needs to come from the bottom."

James grunted. "No. Respect needs to be earned, not given just because I'm tossing you a paycheck."

"You've earned your respect."

"And you've long since earned mine. I'm not 'Mr. Brownstone' to you anymore. I'm James."

"Okay, then, James." Trey grinned. "You're still the boss."

James smirked and nodded to the two other gang members. "These are the two you told me about?"

"Yeah, these boys know what's up. I think they can do a lot more than protect property or collect information. This is Daryl and Isaiah."

James shook both the men's hands. They remained silent, trying a little too hard to look tough.

"And you think they're ready?"

"No, James, I think they have potential." Trey furrowed his brow and looked away. "The problem is, gangbanging involves a lot of fronting. I want to whip the boys into shape—you know, give them real discipline—but now I'm running all over catching bounties. I don't have the time, and I know *you* don't have the time, so I'm trying to figure out what to do."

The men watched James apprehensively. They wanted the job. They wanted something more than being gang members in some shitty neighborhood.

James pulled out his phone. "That's not a problem. I think I got someone who can help."

James pushed into the Far Shores. The dense crowd of people and raucous din reminded the bounty hunter of the Leanan Sídhe, but that was where the resemblance ended.

Photos of soldiers, sailors, airmen, and Marines decorated the wall in the dimly lit main room, along with various military coins. This wasn't a pub. This was a *bar*.

Beyond the décor, the haircuts and builds of the average customer made it clear it was a place frequented by military personnel. The proximity to Camp Pendleton didn't hurt.

Gunnery Sergeant Hawkins waved from a booth in the back, and a young, fit Latina woman sat next to the weathered Marine. James made his way to the booth and took a seat.

"Thanks for meeting me, Gunny," James began. He extended his hand to the woman. "You're Lance Corporal Vasquez, right? From what the gunny told me, you stopped me from taking a sniper round to the head. I asked him to bring you here so I could personally thank you."

The woman gave his hand a firm shake and shrugged. "I just stopped some asshole who was trespassing. No big deal. Just doing my job."

"My brain disagrees." James grinned. "And I kind of like not having it splattered all over the dirt."

Vasquez smirked. "Yeah, that shit sucks."

James looked at the Gunny Hawkins. "Ran into some

Marines in Detroit. They said recruitment was up or some shit because of what happened with the hitmen?"

The gunny nodded. "Yeah, that's what the brass says. Lots of good press over the whole thing. A few people were worried about the active-duty military doing law-enforcement shit on US soil, but those bastards came on to our land, so no legal worries. Hell, even a few medals are getting passed out." He nodded to Vasquez. "She's getting one for catching that sniper."

Vasquez looked down at the table and her face reddened. "It wasn't a big deal. Like I said, just doing my job."

"That guy might not have stopped with me," James told her. "He might have taken a few shots at Marines too. You saved lives that day."

"If you say so," the Marine muttered, her face now scarlet.

Gunny Hawkins chuckled. "So you said you needed some help? Since you're not running from hitmen this time I was curious. What's up?"

"I've got a new business venture, 'the Brownstone Agency.' A bounty hunting company."

The gunny laughed. "I don't know if the world can handle more than one Brownstone."

Vasquez chuckled at that, some of her embarrassment fading.

James shrugged. "It's not a big deal. I don't have the time to deal with a lot of low-level bounties, so I'm trying to hire people who can."

Gunny Hawkins nodded. "Makes sense. But I'm

guessing you don't plan to have your guys trick all those bounties onto Pendleton?"

James snorted. "Nope. That's not the problem. What I need are disciplined men. I need to take them from *thinking* they are tough to actually *being* tough."

"Okay. What do you got to work with?"

James locked eyes with the gunny. "Gangbangers."

Vasquez blinked, but Gunny Hawkins didn't change his expression at all.

"I'm willing to pay good money for someone who can whip them into proper shape rather than just being thugs," James continued, then shrugged. "I figured you might know someone who could help me out with that."

"Yeah, I know a guy. Just got out of the Corps. Spent time as both a recruiter and a drill instructor."

"A drill sergeant. Perfect."

Vasquez and Gunny Hawkins both winced.

James looked between them. "What?"

The gunny pointed to a picture of R. Lee Ermey on a nearby wall. "In the Corps, we have drill instructors. Drill sergeants are an Army thing."

The bounty hunter nodded. "Sorry. Didn't know."

Gunny Hawkins shrugged. "No big deal, and I'd be happy to put you in contact with the guy, especially if you've got money to throw around."

"Like I said, I'm willing to pay well."

The gunny grinned. "Paying better than the Corps isn't hard."

"And you don't think their background is a problem? He won't have a problem training gang members?"

The gunny shook his head. "It's not like every new

recruit we get in the Corps comes from the nicest families. Training is about stripping that shit away and carving a man or woman into something better."

Some emotion flashed in Vasquez's eyes, but James couldn't figure out what was it was.

James shifted his attention to her. "Problem, Vasquez?"

"N-nothing."

"If you've got something to say, go ahead and tell me. I'm fucking hard to offend."

Well, as long as you don't talk shit about my family.

Vasquez sighed, looking down. "It's not like that. It's just...I was in a gang before I joined the Corps. I would have ended up dead in a gutter if it wasn't for the Marine Corps." She looked back up, her face beaming with pride. "Proper discipline can turn *anyone* into someone better, Mr. Brownstone."

"Glad to hear it." James waved down a waitress. "But enough business bullshit for now. How about we have something to drink?"

A couple of hours later as James headed up the highway, his mind ran over everything involved with the Brownstone Agency. The paperwork had been obnoxious, and the idea of managing employees still seemed as mysterious as the World in Between. And now he was having to worry about training people.

This shit is getting complicated. Really fucking complicated.

Despite the difficulties, he hadn't thought of abandoning the agency for more than a few seconds. He could turn the gang into something more disciplined; more useful to both the city and themselves. They could push back against the assholes together, and make good money doing it at the same time.

What do you think, Father Thomas? Am I just fooling myself here, or am I actually doing something good?

He gritted his teeth at the memory of the false Father Thomas the despair bug had conjured in Japan. Even though it was a fiction created by his own mind, the heavy sting of the doppelganger's words lingered.

My ward is a foul-mouthed thug who kills people for a living. And then you inflict your grievous sins on Father McCartney. I wonder how he feels at night having to help you cleanse your disgusting and demon-tainted soul?

He might have killed the monster who fucked with his brain, but that didn't change the truths it had unearthed and the hidden disgust lingering beneath the surface of his mind.

But that didn't matter. He was James Brownstone, and he'd push back against the fucking darkness every damned day until he died. When the time came and he lay bleeding out, he wanted to know he'd taken more evil out of the world than he'd put into it.

The Brownstone Agency was a start, as were Alison and Shay. Friends, family, and a neighborhood to defend. The despair bug had been wrong. James had everything in the world to live for, and everything in the world to protect.

James blew out a long breath. Life wasn't simple anymore, but he no longer thought that was terrible. Annoying as fuck, sure, but not terrible.

He wished he could talk to Shay about it. The tomb

raider knew first-hand what it was like to change from being a loner and start working with other people. Maybe dealing with Peyton wasn't as complicated as trying to train an entire gang, but at least she had some insight.

Fuck. What is it, two more days before my deadline? Where the hell are you that you're out of contact?

His phone chimed in the console and he looked down, his heart rate kicking up at the idea it was Shay.

But Alison, not Shay, had texted him.

Aunt Shay says she is OK and not to worry. She had time to text one person and figured she didn't need to know if you were cooking. She'll call you in 2 days.

James chuckled and then blinked. The timing of the message made him wonder if Alison had access to more magic than he knew.

Coincidence, or is she reading my soul all the way from Virginia?

11

James' phone chimed with a text from Trey.
Getting ready to go after a level one. He's hiding in a motel near Philips Bar-B-Que. Don't you like that place? Heard you mention it a few times.

A smile appeared on the bounty hunter's face. Might as well have a decent lunch and check out Trey in action. He lifted his phone to text back.

Where you at? I'm gonna come pick you up.

Windowmaker smiled and leaned over the table in the bar to emphasize her cleavage. The two uniformed Detroit police officers glanced at each other, then looked back up at her.

The gold wedding bands on both men caught her attention. It'd been a while since she'd harvested two at the same time. Their beer glasses were half-empty so it was a good time to strike, but first she needed to confirm some intelligence.

"Can we help you, Miss?" one of the cops asked. His nametag read Austin.

Widowmaker slipped into a seat and batted her eyelashes at Officer Austin. "Oh, I just love cops, you know? You guys protect this city and make it safe for women like me. Detroit PD has a tough job, and I really appreciate what you do. I can't think of a tougher job than being a cop."

The other cop, Varga, cleared his throat. "Uh, thanks, ma'am."

Her eyes widened and snapped. "Hey, I saw you both on television. When that guy—Greystone, Blackstone, whoever—was on television."

"You talking about Brownstone bringing in that necromancer?" Austin chuckled. "We were just standing in the background. That was an AET and Brownstone show, not a beat-cop thing."

"Oh, come on, now. Fancy AET guys or bounty hunters get all the glory, but you guys are the real line protecting innocents from criminals. I've lived in Detroit all my life, so I know who the real cops are."

Austin shrugged. "Look, all cops do something useful. I got no beef with AET. It's dangerous work."

Varga nodded his agreement. "Yeah, and Lieutenant Walsh is a good guy. He did plenty of time on the streets before joining AET. He doesn't let those guys get cocky and look down on us patrol officers. It's not like that in every city."

Widowmaker stuck out her lip. "I still feel for you, and

what about this Brownstone? He's not even a cop. I'm sure he's sitting in some hotel room now thinking he's so special because he brought in that man. I bet that's annoying to have some bounty hunter taking all the glory."

Varga frowned. "Nah, Brownstone gave half his bounty to the Detroit PD. He didn't have to do that, and because of what he did there's been a huge influx of donations. And not just to AET—the city council's talking about upping the police budget, too. And he's not sitting in some hotel, he's back in LA taking down scumbags there."

The Drow assassin smiled even as she seethed inwardly.

Brownstone is gone? So I've wasted my time. I'll at least harvest these two fools.

"Oh, you guys are as humble as you are brave." The Drow licked her lips. "You know, I've got to admit I've always had a fantasy," she whispered.

"A fantasy?" Vargas blinked. Discomfort spread across his face.

"Yes. Of what it'd be like to be with a cop, but I was kind of wondering what it'd be like to be with *two* cops. I think you guys deserve a little bonus for all you do for the city." She ran a hand down the side of her dress. "And I'd like to be the bonus," she added in a husky voice.

Vargas sighed and scrubbed a hand over his face. "Ma'am, I'm sorry, but I'm Catholic."

Widowmaker snorted and rolled her eyes. "What about you, Officer Austin? I can send you to heaven."

"Yeah, right before my wife sends me to hell." Austin laughed. "No thanks, lady. I'm flattered, but I'm also happily married. And a little scared of my wife."

Vargas laughed this time.

The Drow rose, keeping her smile in place. "You don't know what you're missing. Either of you."

Vargas nodded toward the door. "Ma'am, I think it'd be best if you left."

"If that's what you want." She gave a final coy wink and headed toward the exit.

The Drow walked away from the bar and around the corner into an alley. Annoyance flowed through her veins.

Brownstone always seemed one step ahead of her, as if guarded by some clever spell. If it weren't for all the delicious life she was draining from unfaithful husbands, the mission would have already exceeded the limits of her patience.

She'd been counting on one of the men being unfaithful. It'd been easy so far. *Too* easy. Humans treated their oaths like rotten fruit they were eager to toss away at the first chance.

A scratching noise came from the other end of the alley and the Drow marched toward it, her eyes narrowed.

A wagging tail stuck out from a knocked-over garbage can. A few seconds later, a mangy dog covered in matted fur stepped out, dragging a half-eaten burger patty.

Widowmaker sneered. "You're as disgusting as a human."

The dog dropped its burger and growled at the Drow.

She flicked her wrist and an opaque black sphere shot through the air and struck the dog. He let a howl of pain, collapsing to the ground. The dog rolled around for a few seconds before scampering off as fast as his legs could carry him, his burger left behind. The Drow chuckled, imagining the pain she'd deliver to Brownstone.

"I will destroy you, Brownstone. You may have no vows to dishonor, but you've taken something that isn't yours."

With a deep breath, the Drow reached into her blood and shifted her appearance.

Trey stared out the passenger-side window. "Our boy Jared has been dealing a lot of dust. Might even be able to lead the cops to an important link in the supply chain. Nasty asshole."

James grunted. "And you already have his location. That was quick."

"Yeah. This guy's too cocky, you know what I'm saying? I just had to ask the right people and they gave his ass right up. Turns out being a prick isn't good for business.

James snorted. "Good. If you ever hit a dead end, a good person to start with is Tyler at the Black Sun."

"I haven't been there yet. I've heard of the guy, but never been there. I know they have that neutral shit going on now, but I don't trust that."

James was more than a little suspicious of it himself. He also found it ironic that AET had been a key player in establishing the neutrality.

Guess Hall doesn't give a shit when it's not me.

He checked for suspicious drones or tails before responding. "Tyler hates my ass, but he's honest enough with his information. Really prides himself on being a professional."

"Okay, I'll keep him in mind, but I'm not pretending to be anything other than a bounty hunter with the Brownstone Agency. I'm not gonna take any shit from him about you."

"Good. Stand up to the asshole." James parked his truck across the street from their target motel. "Let's see what you got, Trey."

"Watch and learn, James." Trey winked and stepped out of the truck. "See, you might be James Brownstone, but Trey Garfield brings *style* to this game, you know what I'm saying?"

Trey made his way across the street and toward the target room with a swagger in his step. James followed after a moment but changed course until he stood around the corner from the room.

Trey knocked on the door and waited. "Jared? I'm with the Brownstone Agency. I know you're in there. Why don't you come to the door and save us both some time, okay? We can do the whole hiding-in-the-room shit, but, come on—it's embarrassing to us both."

"You ain't James Brownstone," called the man from the other side of the door. "You think I was gonna fall for that shit?"

"No shit, fucker. I didn't say I was *Brownstone*. I said I work for the Brownstone Agency. Brownstone's my fucking boss, but he doesn't have time to waste on your punk ass. So I'm here to take it in. You gonna come out nicely, or am I gonna have to—"

Two loud shots cut Trey off and sent him flying backward. Bile rose in James' throat as his protégé slammed into the ground.

The bounty hunter sprinted to the door, growling. Two large holes now decorated the door. James didn't stop to think, threaten, or even pull a weapon. He slammed his foot into the door at full strength.

The wood cracked and splintered, and the door sailed inward. Jared yelped and collapsed as it collided with him. His gun, a Desert Eagle, flew out of his hand.

The bounty groaned from the ground and shoved the door off him. His eyes widened.

"You're *fucking James Brownstone!*" Jared screamed.

James yanked the man up and brought back his fist. Jared fainted.

With another growl, the bounty hunter tossed the man to the floor. He spun to find Trey slowly standing up wearing a pained expression.

Trey grimaced. "*Shit* that hurt. I think my ribs are bruised." He looked down. "At least the bastard didn't clip my jacket, just have to replace the tie and shirt. Man, looking good while kicking ass can get expensive. Starting to understand why you dress like that."

James looked down at himself. First Shay, now Trey?

"Wait, why aren't you dead or bleeding out?"

Trey grinned. "Good thing I always use protection. That, and bulletproof vests. I might be a badass, but I ain't motherfucking James Brownstone. I need to be careful." He fished out some handcuffs and headed inside the motel room. "I should beat the motherfucker's ass. He almost killed me."

James grunted but said nothing. Trey was right. If he hadn't been wearing the vest, he might have been dead. He wouldn't begrudge a few sucker punches.

Trey turned Jared over and handcuffed him. "You know what? Fuck that." He sucked in a breath and Smooth Trey returned. "I'm not a hood rat anymore. I'm a professional bounty hunter, and it's not professional to beat down bounties." He nodded to James. "I've got to build the rep of the Brownstone Agency. A good rep can win a fight for you before you've even started. Like the man said, 'Supreme excellence consists of breaking the enemy's resistance without fighting.'"

James frowned. "I've never said that."

Trey laughed. "Not you, James. Sun Tzu. You know, *The Art of War*?"

"Never read it. If the guy wrote a cookbook, I'll get around to reading it eventually. You read ancient Chinese authors?"

"I've been reading a lot of shit since I've started this job." Trey tapped his forehead. "The more you know, the less you die. Anyway, I figure if the word goes out that the Brownstone Agency won't dog on a man once the cuffs are on, more guys will surrender. Don't want them to feel like their backs are against the wall, you know?"

"Sounds like a good plan." James stared down at the unconscious bounty.

Shit. I've always tried to scare assholes into surrendering, but never really thought about how to work it the other way. Maybe Trey's a better businessman than I am.

James grunted. "Let's throw him in the back and swing by the barbeque place for some takeout."

12

James scrolled through the webpage for a restaurant supplier. Even though he didn't have a plan to start his own barbeque restaurant anytime soon, his foray into business had set his mind in motion toward the possibility.

If shit's gonna be complicated anyway, maybe I should think about some of this. It wouldn't be so bad to have a stake in a place. Maybe I could hire someone, but mess around there, too.

He didn't want to run the place himself. He lacked the cooking skills, but he liked the idea of having his own small barbeque kingdom.

If I called it Brownstone's, would that cause trouble or get me business?

James winced, imagining some King Pyro-like asshole blowing open his restaurant and killing a bunch of barbeque lovers.

"Okay, maybe having my own barbeque place wouldn't be a great idea for a few years."

His phone rang and he snatched it from his desk. Shay. His heart beat faster.

"Hello?" James answered, trying to keep the excitement out of his voice.

What the fuck am I doing?

"So, IRS audit your ass yet?"

He chuckled. "It's a new business. I think it takes a little longer than that. You okay?"

"Fuck, yeah. You know me—I'm always okay. I'm leaving Australia to go to Japan. Got another job there, but I'll be back in a week."

"What the fuck were you even doing in Australia that you couldn't call me?"

"Long story short, there's a legend of a ship that came to Australia before Captain Cook—the so-called Mahogany Ship. Turns out the legend's true, and also turns out there were some artifacts aboard. It was kind of an annoying little job tracking the thing down and then some of the other artifacts, and assholes got in my way."

James grunted. "What happened to those assholes? Do I need to have some one-way discussions with people?"

"Nope. I already gave them lead poisoning. There were also several guys with grenade and knife allergies."

James chuckled, but worry ate his mirth. "And you're gonna go on another raid? Shouldn't you rest? Sounds like it was a tougher one than usual."

"Says the man who likes to take down high-level bounties in rapid succession." Shay snorted. "Don't worry, this Japan thing's a milk run." She let out a quiet sigh. "And you're still breathing. That's always good news."

"Yeah, nothing big here. I took down a necromancer in Detroit, but that's about it."

Shay groaned. "Motherfucking zombies."

"Nope, no zombies. This guy hopped bodies."

Shay made a disgusted sound. "That's fucked up and different."

"Don't worry. He was undead, so I just made him dead instead."

"You *are* good at that. Anything else interesting happen?"

James winced. "Shit, there's something I have to admit. I called up Peyton to ask for help on a case. I should have asked you first."

"Peyton's a big boy. Mostly. I don't fucking care if you call him. What did he say when you asked him for help?"

"He made me pay him five thousand dollars."

Shay burst out laughing. "Good to see Peyton is taking care of himself and getting a job. I want to see him mature a little anyway. Now he's Mr. Entrepreneur. Hey, kind of like you! So it's just Trey going around knocking heads so far, or what?"

"Got a couple of other guys we're gonna train up. If things go well, I'll convert the entire gang into bounty hunters and then recruit others."

"Damn, Brownstone! You're gonna run a bunch of other guys out of business."

James snorted. "Only if they're shitty at their jobs."

"Entrepreneur Brownstone. Like my own version of Malibu Barbie or Princess Barbie, but a guy."

"Hey, since you're going to Japan anyway, maybe you could pick me up some *yakiniku*."

Shay laughed. "I don't think it's gonna keep."

"Nah, it's fine. Just pack it in ice. It's the flavor profile I'm interested in anyway."

"'Flavor profile.' Aren't you fancy?" Shay sighed. "That's just my luck. You don't want me, but you still want a piece of meat."

James groaned. "It's not like that."

"It's fine, Brownstone. Don't stress it. I know you like me and I know you've got your issues, so nothing has to happen fast. But I gotta go for now. Got a few things to take care of before I catch my flight. Talk to you later."

"Talk to you later."

Shay hung up.

James stared at the phone. "You light a piece of wood it burns, gives you coal, gives you ash. You talk to a woman, you have no fucking clue which way it will go."

Maria pushed into the Black Sun. She didn't care if the FBI thought Brownstone's assassin floozy was dead. She was more convinced than ever the woman in the picture was the allegedly-dead hitman from New York.

The AET officer made her way straight to the bar, the crowd parting for her. She yanked out her phone, brought up the drone picture, and held it up to Tyler. Kathy glanced their way but didn't come over for a closer look.

"Good evening to you too, Lieutenant," Tyler greeted her with a smirk.

"I'm not in a good mood. Do you know this woman? I

know it's not the best picture, but if you have any sort of clue, I need to know who she is. This is important shit."

Tyler stared at the picture, his brow creasing. "As much as it pains me to admit this, I have no idea who this woman is. Not even the slightest."

"Are you sure? Because if I find her, I'll be able to piss off Brownstone big time."

The bartender smiled and leaned forward again for another look.

Maria snickered. "Yeah, I figured that would motivate you."

Tyler's smile slowly turned into a frown. "Damn, I'm sorry. You know how I love to do my civic duty when it comes to Brownstone, but I really have no clue."

Maria took a deep breath. "You're not shitting me, are you? This isn't some sort of power play or manipulation? I need this woman. She's the key to taking down Brownstone."

Tyler shook his head, irritation in his eyes. "Nope. No clue, and it's pissing me off because not only do I not like being ignorant, I don't like the idea I can't fuck over Brownstone when handed an opportunity by a cop, of all people."

The lieutenant muttered a few obscenities and pocketed her phone. "Don't worry, you'll get your chance. It's just a matter of when."

I'm not giving up yet, Brownstone. Your ass is still mine.

James folded his hands in front of him as he waited for his

guest. He wasn't sure if having a meeting at a barbeque restaurant was all that professional, but he didn't give much of a shit. The Brownstone Agency was never going to be fancy, and everyone who worked for him needed to accept that up front.

A huge and muscled middle-aged dark-haired man with closely-cropped hair in a tight t-shirt and jeans stepped in, his every movement radiating confidence and precision. He walked straight to James' table.

"I'm Staff Sergeant Chris Royce." He grunted. "Make that Staff Sergeant Chris Royce, retired."

James stood and shook his hand. "James Brownstone." He pointed to a tray of ribs and pitcher of beer already on the table. "Help yourself. You want me to call you Staff Sergeant?"

"Chris or Royce is fine."

"Most people call me Brownstone, but I don't really give a shit what people call me."

Royce chuckled and slid into a seat. "So Gunny and your email said you needed a man to whip some men into shape?"

James nodded. "Yeah, that at first, but it's gonna go beyond that. I want someone who can handle recruiting new people, training new people, and, fuck, I guess staff management or whatever you want to call it for a lot of guys with a lot of testosterone. I've really only got one guy working for me now, but I'm an ass-kicker, not a leader."

Royce eyed James, curiosity on his face. "I'm not a bounty hunter. I've been a Marine my whole life. You sure you want a guy like me around? I'm all about discipline, not following your gut or whatever shit.."

"I don't need you to be a bounty hunter. You're *exactly* what I want. I need you to instill discipline in new recruits. If I'm gonna grow this company, I can't have a bunch of thugs going out there and causing trouble. My name's attached and my rep's attached, which means it's my responsibility. You get my men disciplined, able to shoot and hit shit, and throw a punch. Trey and I can help them figure out the investigation part."

Royce picked up a rib. "Gunny also mentioned that your first group of candidates are a bunch of sad-sack piece-of-shit gang members."

James grunted. "Yeah, do you have a problem with that? These guys working for me is non-negotiable. If they can't handle the training that's one thing, but they're getting the chance."

Royce shrugged. "I dealt with more than my share of gang members who joined the Corps. And these punks have you to look up to, so it makes it easier." He took a bite from the rib. "Good barbeque."

"Yeah, it is good barbeque, and I'm no role model."

"Yeah, you're just a guy who was on TV taking out an entire gang. A guy other cities call to come and kick ass for them." The Marine chuckled. "Just saying it's a good thing, Brownstone. In the Corps it's easy. You have flag and country to point the kids toward. Since you're a private guy it's a little harder, so we need a new symbol. *You're* that fucking symbol, whether you like it or not. Men always need someone to rally around, and you're the fucking man in charge—and unlike a lot of generals, you can personally kick ass. If you can't handle a little attention, this isn't gonna work."

"I get that." James gave a shallow nod. "You do whatever you need to do...assuming you're interested." He polished off a rib.

He didn't like the idea of being a symbol of anything, but he wasn't about to tell a Marine Corps DI how to do his job.

"That offer you sent me in the email still stands?" Royce asked.

"Yeah."

"That's some damned good pay. Very generous."

"Pay for the best, you get the best. Besides, I'm not a stingy guy."

The Marine reached for the pitcher of beer and poured himself a glass. "I've gotta take care of some shit over the next week, but after that, I'm ready to start. Where are we going to be doing this?"

James thought that over for a second.

Shit. That asshole banker was right. I am *going to need a building, after all.*

"Royce, why don't you tell me what you need and I'll buy a building."

The Marine put down his beer and grinned. "Damn, I wish it had been that easy in the Corps."

13

James pushed into the Leanan Sídhe, every muscle in his body tense. He still owed the Professor his participation in a Bard of Filth competition, and every stop in the Irish pub brought a greater risk of being forced to humiliate himself with a filthy song or limerick.

Fuck. I shouldn't have borrowed those artifacts. I don't know if it was really worth it in the end. Damn it.

The bounty hunter wanted to avoid a repeat of the awkwardness in Detroit. He didn't mind a few good obscenities, but he didn't get the appeal of ribald cadences or filthy limericks, and he didn't think he ever would.

Sex wasn't fucking funny.

And he certainly didn't want to risk some asshole recording the whole thing and spreading it over the internet, especially when he was trying to build up the reputation of the Brownstone Agency.

The Professor's earlier call asking James to stop by the

pub hadn't mentioned the contest, but the man wasn't above a little deception if he thought it'd be funny.

James gritted his teeth as he made his way to the Professor's booth in the back. More than a few people glanced his way, but he wasn't sure if that was because they wanted him to hear him spew out nasty limericks or because of his recent appearances on the news.

The bounty hunter grunted as he slid in across from the Professor. "Hey, Professor."

To James' surprise, the older man wasn't red-faced, and his single glass of beer looked all but untouched. Tension furrowed his face.

The bounty hunter frowned. The Professor rarely showed any signs of being worried much about anything. James had become convinced the man would laugh his way through the Apocalypse while drinking the Four Horsemen under the table.

"Good evening, lad." The Professor managed a pained smile. "Thank you for coming."

"You said you had something important and urgent for me to handle?"

"Aye, I've got a little job opportunity for you. It's something I'd ask Miz Carson to do, but alas, she's out of the country." The Professor shrugged. "But the more I think about it, the more I think you're better suited for this sort of thing."

"Wait, you mean like a tomb raid?" James shook his head. "You don't want me even trying that shit other than running support. I don't know all that history and shit like she does."

The Professor frowned and took a very small sip of his

beer. "It's not a tomb raid. It's more a pick-up and delivery job. That is to say, another tomb raider has already collected an item for me; a small blue jewel, using all that knowledge of history and shit, as you put it. All I need you to do is go to Seattle to pick it up and bring it back to me."

"Why can't the tomb raider bring it himself?"

"He was sloppier than he should have been and now other people are aware that he brought the artifact to Seattle. These other people, lad, are simply much more lethal than he is. He's a good raider, but not much of a fighter. The nature of the artifact also makes it hard to hide from certain types of locator spells when it's moving for more than a couple of hours." The Professor shrugged. "He's at a place where he can't be tracked, but it won't protect him or the artifact forever."

James grunted. "So why not just hop on a supersonic flight and zoom here? He could get it here in a little over an hour then, and you can stick it wherever you hide shit."

"Ah, if only it were so simple." The Professor chuckled quietly. "The problem is that artifact can't be flown anywhere. For various magical reasons I won't bore you with, if the artifact is taken too far from the ground, it'll explode."

"Fucking magic. Is it ever *not* obnoxious?" James shook his head.

"It gets better, lad."

"Better?"

The Professor gave a solemn nod. "The explosion wouldn't be small. Let's just say we don't want it to happen near any populated areas. It'd be inconvenient for the people who live there. And the plants. And all the animals."

James scrubbed a hand over his face. "You're fucking kidding me. What the hell is this thing, and why did you have this guy dig it up?"

"An ancient and extremely potent Atlantean power crystal. And I had him dig it up because other people were looking for it, people with much less restraint than I practice even when I'm ten beers in."

James sighed. "Power crystal, huh? What does that mean? What does it actually do?"

"One could easily imagine its use as a weapon, but it's not actually that by nature. It's less what it can do than what it can fuel. The full return of magic has amplified the risks proportionately." The Professor leaned in and lowered his voice, weariness infusing it. "This isn't something we need in circulation, lad, even among so-called good people. I have my own means of blocking tracking once I receive the artifact. Unfortunately, it can't be sent directly to the World in Between using any of the artifacts I have access to, but I can at least manage to keep it away from prying eyes and hands. The important thing in the meantime is keeping it away from anyone else."

James blew out a long breath, now understanding why the Professor seemed tense—something as rare as seeing him totally sober. There was nothing that could ruin your day like learning a magical nuke was sitting in Seattle and could go off if someone wasn't careful about how they transported it.

"Shit, sounds like my kind of job. Don't even have to fly. I hit the 5, I can get there in a day." James cleared his throat. "So, about payment. Maybe we could strike a deal."

Something approaching amusement reappeared on the Professor's face. "A deal, lad?"

"You know, if I do this, then I don't have to do your Bard of Filth Competition?"

The older man laughed and wagged a finger. "No, no, no, lad. You're still doing that. I've been nice. I've just been trying to give you time so you won't totally embarrass yourself. The Bard of Filth is a contest of true talent, not just bawdy nonsense."

"I can't do that shit. I've been trying to get some help writing the limericks, but I've got nothing so far. Come *on*."

"The Sword of Damocles always falls eventually, James. Make sure you're ready. I'll owe you a big favor or three for this job, but I can't give up the Bard of Filth competition."

"Seriously?"

The Professor laughed. "There are only two things in life I'm always serious about, James: beer and filthy limericks."

James grunted. "Fuck. It was worth a try." He rose. "Okay, I'm in. I'm gonna go hit my warehouse and get the shit I need. Sounds like I should hit the road as soon as I fucking can."

"You're doing me a major favor that I won't soon forget."

"Yeah, but you're still not letting me out of your dirty limerick shit. That's some bullshit."

The Professor smiled and gulped down some beer. He exhaled loudly. "Some things are even more important than the safety of the world, James."

Widowmaker stepped into the Leanan Sídhe with a smile on her face. She'd reverted to her young Angelina Jolie look, having taken a liking to the form. Her latest information from the Black Sun suggested Brownstone might come to the pub, but she needed to confirm that it wasn't another false trail.

She surveyed the packed room but failed to spot the distinctive bounty hunter. A sense of familiarity settled over her; a hunter's instinct honed over a long time.

I can almost smell you, James Brownstone. Were you here? Were you close?

The Drow strolled toward the bar, several men watching her as she moved. She instinctively searched for wedding bands, marking a few potential harvests for later. Her mission awaited.

The bartender offered her a smile. "What'll it be, miss?"

"I'm looking for someone. I was told I might be able to find him here." She played with a lock of her hair. "It's important that I find him."

"Lots of people like this place." He gestured to the crowd. "Who is it you're looking for?"

"James Brownstone."

The bartender chuckled. "Should have figured. We get a few of you groupie types snooping around in here whenever he's on TV lately. Anyway, you just missed him. He was here not ten minutes ago. Sorry."

Widowmaker matched his chuckle, even though she wanted to rip out his life energy in frustration. *So close.*

"Oh." She let out a light sigh. "Do you know where he might be going? I'm not a groupie. This is about business… his business. Bounty hunting."

"You're a bounty hunter?" Incredulity crept onto the man's face.

"Oh, no. I have some information for Mr. Brownstone on a bounty." She leaned forward and lowered her voice. "I'm an informant."

The bartender gestured to a booth in the back where a white-haired middle-aged human sat drinking a beer. "Father O'Banion might be able to help you. He was the last one to talk to him."

Widowmaker smiled. "Thank you."

She rose and walked straight to the booth. She didn't bother to ask his permission as she sat across from him and folded her hands in front of her.

Something tugged at the edge of her consciousness. Her skin tingled, and her heart pounded. This human was much more than he appeared. Dangerous, even. Nothing about his puffy-faced appearance and portly middle suggested an obvious danger, but the Drow assassin traded in false impressions and knew never to place naïve trust in what one saw.

I'll just get the information about Brownstone and harvest this one to be safe. Laena will understand. Our mission is too important.

"I'm sorry to bother you, Father." The Drow tilted her head, looking the man up and down. "You don't...look much like a priest, if you don't mind me saying."

"Ah, not a priest, madam." The man laughed. "I'm still Smite-Williams for now. I've not drunk nearly enough for Father O'Banion to come out."

The Drow furrowed her brow, confusion adding to her

annoyance. What an annoying human. She would enjoy harvesting him later.

"Very well, Mr. Smite-Williams."

He grinned. "Doctor Smite-Williams, actually."

Widowmaker let out a quiet chuckle, but the back of her neck tingled. Was the human taunting her on purpose?

His punishment can wait. I need to get him to tell me where Brownstone is.

"I'm sorry, Doctor," the Drow replied quietly. "I was just looking for James Brownstone. I need his help, and I was told you could point me in his direction."

"Poor thing. You just missed him, madam. Would you be interested in a drink with me instead?"

The Drow shook her head. "No, I really need to find Mr. Brownstone. It's important. Very important."

Smite-Williams sighed. "It always is with him." He chuckled. "Well, you're a lot nicer on the eyes than the last pair looking for him."

"He needs to hear what I'm going to tell him as soon as possible. I…need to tell him in person. I can't risk a message."

The human gave her a toothy grin. "'Need' is such an odd concept. We use that word all the time and it implies so much, but what does it really mean? You see… What was your name again?"

"Angie."

"But of course it is." Amusement shone on the man's face. "Well, Angie, I think James is busy for the next few days. Maybe you could stop off in a week or so and ask around for him. Tomorrow, he could be back here, or he could be in Mexico for all I know. Or Japan. He took a trip there recently. Ate a lot of meat, killed a psychic monster. Standard tourist stuff."

Widowmaker let out a pained laugh. "Oh, come on, Doctor. You strike me as a man who knows what's going on around LA and with James Brownstone."

"I know what's going on if it involves beer, aye. Otherwise, I'm just simple academic." Smite-Williams shrugged. "Sorry, Angie."

"Maybe…we could work a deal of some sort." She beamed a smile at him.

Smite-Williams leaned forward, an eager gleam in his eyes. "I like deals. What did you have in mind?"

Widowmaker smirked. She had him now.

"Maybe an exchange of…fluids."

"An exchange of fluids?" He grinned. "I definitely like the sound of that."

"Yes, so do I." Widowmaker licked her lips.

"Can I pick the fluids?"

"Oh, most definitely, Doctor. I'll also let you pick the place for the exchange."

The human's gaze roamed her body for a moment and the Drow stopped the triumphant laugh that wanted to escape. This man had fallen prey to her charms with so little effort. It was almost disappointing.

Smite-Williams' gaze bore into her now, the intensity almost unnerving. "Do you swear, Angie, that I can pick the fluids and the place?"

"Oh, yes." She put a hand on her chest and gave him a seductive smile.

The human slammed his hand on the table and grinned, all the intensity gone from his face. "Fine, then. Let's play a nice little game. You're going to pay for the next two drinks, and I'm going to tell the waitress to tell the bartender to surprise us. I reserve the right to exchange my drink with you here at this table if I don't like the first one."

"I..." Widowmaker smirked. Nothing about what he said violated their agreement. "Okay, but what do I get out of this little deal?"

"Maybe a good drink, but I already gave you something."

"What?"

"Now you know James stops around this place, which is what I think you wanted to know to begin with." He lifted his hand to flag down a waitress. "Now, let's drink, Angie. Maybe I'll get drunk enough that Father O'Banion can come out, and you can make a deal with him, too. Just let me warn you, he's far quicker than Professor Smite-Williams."

Widowmaker offered him a thin smile. Smite-Williams had beat her. She'd have her drink and leave, even if she longed to choke him with a shadow tentacle.

The man was right about one thing. She now had at least one location to find Brownstone.

Soon I will find others.

14

James was just about to roll away from his warehouse when he received a text from the Professor.

He drove his F-350 back to the pub and stepped inside, hurrying toward the back and not even caring he was in one of his now standard-issue shabby gray coats and armed to the teeth. Anyone who was a regular at the pub knew better than to fuck with him whether or not he was loaded for the job.

The Professor patted a suitcase with a DNA lock. "I thought of something that might be helpful." He pushed the briefcase toward James. "This won't make things simpler, but it does up the chances of that artifact getting to me in one piece and without taking any cities with it."

James grunted. "Yeah, I like things simple, but it's been a long time since that's been the case so I'll fucking deal." His gaze flicked to the case. "So what's inside?"

"Two artifacts I've borrowed from an old friend. I got

lucky and they were available on short notice." The Professor tapped the briefcase. "Check your email. I figured it'd be efficient to have the instructions in there for you. I've set some other things up in Seattle that'll also be handy, assuming you do what I think you'll do with these artifacts."

James pulled out his phone and scanned the email. "Huh. These *could* be handy." The bounty hunter grinned. "I think I've got a halfway-decent plan now; a lot better than just, 'Kill everyone who runs into me.'"

"I knew you would say that." The Professor gave him a little salute. "And you do what you need to do to guarantee that object's safety."

James furrowed his brow. "If you have these anyway, do you really need me to do it?"

"Aye. Even in the best scenario this still ends with a lot of people attacking someone, and I know few people better at returning violence than you."

James snorted. "That's one way to put it."

"The truth is, I've asked for your assistance because there's no one else I trust to handle this situation. You've proven yourself more than a few times, and I know you care about more than just money and bounties no matter *what* you try to claim at times."

"Fuck." James grabbed the suitcase and stood. "Well, I've got a two-day drive ahead of me, so I should get going. I want to get this shit over with before Shay gets back."

"One last thing before you go, lad. It's probably not important, but I figured it'd be best to mention it to you."

"What? Some Harriken dudes who were hiding out on

Oriceran have reappeared to swear vengeance on me or some shit?"

The Professor chuckled and shook his head. "Nothing like that...I think, at least. Have you pissed off any beautiful women lately? Ones who look like a young Angelina Jolie?"

James imagined the actress in his mind and shrugged. "Not that I know of, but maybe they were the girlfriend of some asshole I killed or brought in. It's not like I interview every asshole I take down."

"A lover? That's a strong possibility. Anyway, such a woman was looking for you, and I don't think it was to give you a kiss. Be aware of that for when you come back."

"Whatever. I'll deal with that shit when I get back. One problem at a time."

"That's one way to keep life simpler."

James stifled a yawn as he knocked on the townhouse door and looked up into the camera above the door.

"You know why I'm here. I've driven two days. Let's hurry this shit up before someone gets stupid ideas and drops a bomb on you."

The door clicked open and an exhausted-looking middle-aged man in glasses nodded for James to enter.

"You Henry?" James stepped inside. The lack of furniture other than a small folding table and a metal chair suggested a hastily-arranged safehouse.

"Yeah." Henry closed the door. "Thanks for agreeing to

do this. This shit's going to be a little too 'Mad Max' for me to handle. But you're James Brownstone, so you know all about how to handle crazy thugs trying to murder you on the road. You're a damned *expert* at it."

James shrugged. "I live a colorful life. Not gonna deny that."

The tomb raider gestured to a briefcase on an end table. "It's in there. A lot of people are going to be coming after you for that." He sucked in a breath. "I should have never agreed to recover it, but the money was too good. My ex-wife always said greed was going to get me killed."

"Life's a bitch, then you die. Don't worry. It's not gonna be your problem anymore." James picked up the briefcase. "I figure there's not a lot of point to sitting around chatting about this shit unless you have something to tell me that the Professor didn't."

Henry locked eyes with James. "This might be too much, even for you. Some serious people want this. Understand that."

"You don't know me that well, but there's no one more fucking serious than me. Just ask the Harriken or Jacob Leesom." James smirked. "But, hey, you might be right. You want to keep it? I'll just hit some barbeque places and head back. Enjoy your city-destroying Atlantean artifact."

Henry shook his head and waved his hands in front of him. "No, just saying you should be careful. And whatever you do, do *not* fly with that thing. You'll take a lot of people with you if you do."

"Yeah, the Professor made that pretty fucking clear. As for being careful…" James shrugged. "It's the other guys who should be careful. I haven't had a decent workout in a while. This might be fun."

An hour later James pulled into the parking lot of an Ivar's. He wasn't there to buy fish. It wasn't that he *never* ate fish, but he preferred his food to be sourced from four legs and the land. Or at a minimum, two legs and mostly the land.

Somehow that struck him as more natural. Animals that lived on land should eat animals that lived on land, and animals that lived in the sea should eat animals that lived in the sea. He remained undecided on the true nature of birds, especially chicken with Alabama white sauce slathered over it.

Not like most birds live off eating other birds. I think they count as land animals.

A black Porsche pulled up beside his truck and a beautiful young Asian woman in a body-hugging sheath dress and sunglasses stepped out of it. Her bright green-dyed hair contrasted with the color of her car.

She sauntered to his window. A huge orange purse hung over her shoulder, and James wondered if she had a gun or three in there. Probably a few grenades. He could see the advantage of a purse in situations where you needed to hide a lot of weapons—not that he was going to start carrying one.

The woman lowered her sunglasses. One eye was blue, the other green. That matched the description of James' contact, according to the Professor's email, but that still left the passphrase—words that brought bile into James' throat.

Fucking Professor. Sometimes I want to smash that smug fucking smile off your face.

"You're Addie?" the bounty hunter rumbled.

"We're not having a conversation until you say what I'm expecting to hear." The woman covered her eyes again with her sunglasses. "So say what you need to say, big boy."

James grunted. "Seriously, I have to say that shit? It's not like there are a lot of other people who look like me. You know who I fucking am."

The woman snorted. "Yeah, because in a world filled with magic it's completely impossible that anyone could fake their appearance. The possibility boggles my tiny brain." She crossed her arms. "Verification. That's the way I work. You've got ten seconds, then I walk. You try anything funny and neither of us will like the results."

The bounty hunter stared at the woman, his face tight. Her hand lingered near the top of her purse.

James had no doubts that any sudden movements would result in a gun battle.

"Eight seconds," she said. "Seven seconds. Six seconds."

Fuck you, Smite-Williams. Fuck you with a rusty nail for making me do this.

James took a deep breath and opened his mouth.

"There was an old man from Detroit
Whose dick was remarkably short.
When he got into bed
His old woman said,
This isn't a prick, it's a wart."

James facepalmed. "Fucking Professor. I hate you."

The passphrase limerick was part of the Professor's twisted idea for training James for the Bard of Filth competition. It was also proof that there was no way the bounty hunter was escaping that looming disaster.

"Verified." Addie smirked and pulled a square metallic plate from her purse. "Need DNA confirmation as well."

"If you were gonna do *that*, why did I need to do the fucking limerick?"

The woman shrugged. "Multi-factor authentication. I know you're used to punching people who annoy you through walls and blowing up their buildings, but us non-Scourge of Harriken types need to be more careful. Now, give me your finger or I walk."

James pressed a finger to the DNA scanner and waited for the familiar burning sensation.

The woman's phone chimed in her purse. "Verified. Thanks, Mr. Brownstone. Yeah, I'm Addie Endo. I've already received my payment from my primary client, so I can help you per the instructions I've already received and agreed to, but if you want to change the plan *he'll* need to contact me. Not you. That's the way I work. If you don't like it, you can walk."

"Not a problem. The plan's fine as is."

"You sure about this? Even with my help, you're still going to have a lot of heat on your ass for the next couple of days."

"And how is that different from any other week for me? At least my house didn't get blown up."

Addie laughed. "I like you, Mr. Brownstone." She rubbed her hands together, her eyes filled with eagerness. "Let's do this thing!"

James emerged from the AM/PM with beef jerky in a bag. Now that the retrieval plan was fully in motion, he was going to drive to LA over a two-day period. He wondered if he should be walking around with the briefcase handcuffed to his wrist or something.

He'd considered doing a straight one-day drive, but being exhausted while trying to fend off potential attacks seemed like a bad idea. Not only that, but unlike when he was fleeing the Harriken, he couldn't rely on many of the roads being cleared. He might have to worry about traffic.

James had already taken the time to look up some of the best barbeque places along his route and sampled more than a few on the way up, but he planned to sleep in a rest stop, parked away from anyone else. A hotel or motel presented too many opportunities for a rocket launcher to inflict collateral damage.

It wasn't a bad deal, overall. It'd be a fun little road trip, just with a lot more explosions and bullets.

Two smoking men pushed away from the wall and dropped their cigarettes to the ground.

Fucking assholes. There's an ashtray on the garbage can just ten feet away.

James slowed his pace. The men's stances lacked the looseness he'd expect of two buddies finishing cigarettes. Tension creased their necks and faces.

The men strode toward James with hostility in their eyes. Their hands dropped to their pants pockets, but he didn't see a gun bulge.

James switched the bag to his left hand and the men pulled out switchblades, which extended with a click.

"Where is it?" one of the men asked. "Just give it to us, asshole, and you don't get hurt."

"You're fucking kidding me, right?" James snorted. "This shit is almost insulting."

The men glared at him and their nostrils flared.

"I don't give two shits that you're pissed." James shook his head. "Let me guess: you're some sort of idiot subcontractors. Some asshole's giving you what you think is a big payday, like, I don't know, a thousand dollars or some shit. Here's the problem—I also guarantee you that fucker is probably watching and is just using you to feel me out because you're disposable."

The men's faces tightened. "You're gonna get hurt, freak."

"Nah. Don't do it, assholes. You're the ones who are gonna get hurt. It's almost not worth my time to beat your asses down."

"Fuck you." The man nodded toward his partner. "Just finish his ass and we'll take his keys. Got to hurry before any cops show up."

Fuck it. I gave them their chance.

James took a plodding step forward, then another. The second man charged. Without dropping his bag of beef jerky, the bounty hunter slammed his free fist into the attacker's face.

Blood sprayed from his nose and he smashed against the hard brick wall of the building before falling to the ground, unconscious.

The other man stabbed at James, but the bounty hunter

dodged and grabbed his wrist. He bent it back until the bones snapped, and the man screamed. Another wall toss finished off his assailant.

"Pathetic," James rumbled. He wiped his bloodied knuckles off on the bag and continued toward his truck.

None of these fuckers better jump me at a barbeque place. If they do, I will fucking end *them.*

15

James pushed into the little hole-in-the-wall barbeque place. There were only six tables in the room, and the decor focused more on plastic tablecloths than elegant atmosphere. Photos of happy customers lined the wall, along with a few framed awards from local and regional barbeque competitions.

The short old woman sitting behind the front counter smiled. "Welcome to The Fire Pit. Take a seat wherever you want."

James nodded politely and headed toward a table in the back corner. He wanted to be able to see outside in case someone decided to ambush him.

A picture caught his eye. He leaned in to inspect it. A smiling Elf woman stood next to the old woman from the counter, making a V sign with her hand.

"Hey, isn't this Nadina?"

James hadn't read anything to suggest she'd come through Tumwater, Washington on any of her tours.

The owner nodded. "She came here a few years back. Talked about wanting to sample all the best barbeque in each state. We don't get a lot of Oricerans in here." A warm smile spread across her face. "I knew even then that she'd do something special."

James sat and grabbed a menu off the table. "Give me five pounds of the House Special ribs."

"Sure thing, hon." After taking a few steps toward the back door, the woman spun and stared at James.

He shifted in his seat under her attention. "What?"

"You're James Brownstone. *The* James Brownstone."

"Yeah." He shrugged. "I like barbeque."

The woman clapped. "This is perfect. With Nadina, she wasn't a celebrity yet, but you're already a celebrity. Can I take a picture of you for our wall?"

James grunted. "Sure, but I'm not a celebrity."

"You've been on TV more than I have." The woman laughed. "So, you ordered the House Special ribs. Is Memphis style your favorite?"

James shrugged. "I don't know. I used to say Carolina styles, but now I don't know. I've always loved all types of barbeque."

"Oh? Something change your mind about the Carolinas?"

"All this Nadina stuff and a recent trip to Japan has got me thinking I shouldn't limit myself that way. It's like every time we taste barbeque, we're tasting one tiny piece of the ultimate barbeque flavor but missing so much. Only by trying all possible barbeque can we approach knowing what the essence of true barbeque is." James sighed. "Does that make sense?"

The woman nodded slowly. "Oh, hon, it makes perfect sense."

"Joe!" the woman shouted. "Get out here. We've got a celebrity and he's a true barbeque lover, not some faker."

An old man emerged from the door leading to the kitchen. "Damn." His eyes widened. "James Brownstone." He leaned forward, looking the bounty hunter up and down. "Those muscles are even bigger than they look on television. You could carry my entire grill with one of those arms."

James chuckled.

"Get the phone and let's take some pictures," the old woman ordered. "We're going to put his picture right next to Nadina's."

James finished off another rib as he continued listening to Mary, the owner, explain the twenty-year history of her restaurant.

"So that's how we ended up going more with a Memphis style after focusing on Texas style for so many years. Sorry, we don't really do any Carolina stuff here."

"Not a big deal. Like I said, I love it all."

"How about you, James? What got you started on your love of barbeque?"

James blinked. He'd not thought a lot about that through the years. Very few people had ever bothered to ask him—not that anyone would have bothered until recently. No one had gotten that close.

"I was raised in a Catholic orphanage," he explained.

"There was a priest who was like a second father to me. Father Thomas."

James almost snorted. He'd let his memories of the priest be tainted by pain for so many years, a weakness the despair bug had attempted to exploit in Japan, but all lives had both pain and joy. He needed to remember the latter and not always focus on the former.

"This priest was into barbeque?" Mary asked.

"Yeah. Now that I think of it, all my earliest barbeque memories involve him. He liked Carolina styles, so I guess that's why I've preferred them. I still remember the first time I smelled that delicious meat on the grill. My mouth watered and I wanted to run down there right away, but Father Thomas wouldn't let us eat until everything was ready and we'd said grace." James picked up a rib and stared at it, pleasant memories from long ago flooding into him. "It's not like the orphanage could afford to do that sort of thing a lot, so it became a special-occasion event. It taught me that barbeque meant warmth and family, even when you didn't have any." He shook his head. "Sorry. Shit, didn't mean to get all weird."

"No," Mary argued. "That was beautiful. I've never met anyone who understands the power of food and barbeque like you, James. You ever consider giving up your dangerous job and opening your own place?"

He chuckled. "Yeah, eventually. Not for a few years yet. I'm still a dabbler, not a real barbeque man."

The woman wagged a finger. "You're more of a real barbeque man than ninety-five percent of the so-called 'barbeque men' out there." Her eyes widened. "Hey, what are you doing in Washington, anyway?" She dropped her voice to a whisper. "Are there some gangsters you're going after in Tumwater?"

James managed to not laugh in her face. "Nope. Just doing a little barbeque road trip."

"Just like Nadina!"

"Yeah, something like that." James glanced up at a clock. "I better get going. I have a pretty tight schedule. Thanks for the food and conversation."

Mary stood. "Let me get you some ribs for the road. It's on the house."

Well, at least no one fucked with me while I was here.

James yawned as he approached Exit 39 leading to Kelso, Washington. His Tumwater stop for barbeque had taken care of his fuel, but his truck needed gas.

A red and blue light flashed in his rearview mirror and he glanced in the rearview mirror to see an unmarked Crown Victoria.

The bounty hunter frowned. He hadn't been speeding and there wasn't a single dent on the F-350, let alone a broken taillight. He'd spent enough money repairing the truck after the Harriken bounty to ensure that.

James grunted, slowed, and pulled to the shoulder, resting his hands on the wheel after rolling his window down. Traffic stops could be tense for cops, given they never knew if they were going to get a soccer mom or a murderer in the front seat. He didn't want to make any cop's day tougher.

A plainclothes cop with a crew-cut and a brown leather jacket emerged from the car and walked toward the F-350.

James kept his hands atop of the wheel. "How can I help you, officer?"

"Got a call over the radio about a vehicle matching your description with some drugs. I'm going to need to ask you to get out of your car, sir."

"Don't you need my license and registration first?" James chuckled. "Or do you already know who I am?"

The cop's hand jerked up. His coat swished, revealing a shoulder holster. "You need to slowly get out of the car. I don't have any idea who you are, asshole. I just know there's a report about drugs in your car. So get the fuck out and don't make any sudden movements."

James didn't dare blink. "I'd like to see your badge and police ID card, please, Officer."

"Fuck this." The man reached into his jacket.

James slammed his door into the man and he went down with a grunt. The bounty hunter was on him in seconds, throwing him onto his stomach and pinning his arms behind him.

"You're attacking a police officer, asshole," the man snarled. "You better get the fuck off me if you know what's good for you."

"Nah, I think you're a piece of shit who is impersonating a police officer. I'm gonna call the cops right now, then we'll see what's what."

The man squirmed but didn't accomplish much other than annoying James.

A loud siren cried from down the road, red-and-blue lights flashing. A highway patrol call screeched to a halt about ten seconds later and the wide-brimmed state trooper stepped out of his car, his gun already out.

This time the marked car and uniform convinced James of the identity of the new arrival. He rose slowly, his hands up.

James nodded toward the man on the ground. "This guy's impersonating a cop."

"You're going to jail, asshole." The man on the ground hopped to his feet. "This Brownstone douchebag has about a good thirty kilos of dust in this truck. Cuff his ass."

"Huh." James chuckled. "Before you said you didn't know who I am."

The state trooper kept his gun up. "I think I need both of you to turn around and put your hands on your heads while I sort this out. Don't make any sudden movements."

The other man sneered and turned away from James, and the movement lifted his coat again, revealing a second holster—not for a gun, but for a thin wooden wand.

Shit.

The wizard snatched his wand and pointed it at the cop. *"Magna ig—"*

James' right hook smashed into the wizard's head and the man spun like a top, his wand sailing into the road. A passing car ran over it, snapping it in half.

The trooper glanced at James and the fallen wizard, his gun still out.

The bounty hunter raised his hands again and laced them behind his head. His amulet might be on his chest, but it was still separated from contact. He was still tough without it, but he wasn't bulletproof.

"Damn, was that what I thought it was?" the trooper asked.

"Yeah. Wand."

"I think the nearest AET team is in Portland."

James grunted. "A guy like that can't channel power without a wand." He nodded toward the fragments of the wand. "He's just another douchebag for now."

"Hey, wait." The trooper holstered his firearm. "You're James Brownstone."

"Yeah, I am. And I'm guessing there's no report out there with a vehicle matching my description carrying drugs?"

The trooper shook his head. "Nope."

"Can I put my hands down now?"

"Yeah, go ahead." The trooper knelt to cuff the unconscious wizard. "Hey, can you do me a favor?"

"What?"

"My kid would love it if I could get an autograph from you. He's always complaining about how I don't have any funny celebrity stories."

James grunted. "I'm not a celebrity."

"But you've been on—"

"Television more than you have." James sighed. "Sure. Mind if I sign a business card?"

"Bounty hunters have business cards?"

"It's for my agency—the Brownstone Agency."

"Oh. That sounds great."

Someone whispered near the Crown Victoria, but James didn't see anyone. He leapt forward, tackling the very surprised trooper. Two bolts of lightning blasted through the air, one where James had been standing a second before and the other right over the downed bounty hunter and trooper.

James rolled off the trooper and scrambled toward the cop's car. The trooper rushed after him and they both made it to cover as another blast of lightning zapped the car. Sparks shot from it, and the vehicle died, along with the lights.

"You okay?" The bounty hunter whipped out his .45. "Sorry, I know I hit hard."

"Fuck, you just saved my life."

James peered around the front of the car. The air shimmered near the Crown Victoria. He squeezed off several rounds, but he didn't hear any screams of pain.

"Several more units on the way already from when I first stopped," the trooper said. "But they are about ten minutes out still."

"I'm gonna run for my car and draw his attention. You shoot at where the lightning's coming from."

"That's an insane plan."

James shrugged. "That's how the Brownstone Agency rolls. Okay, on one…two…three."

He sprinted toward his truck and another blast of lightning zipped by him, the heat warming the back of his neck. He leapt behind his F-350 as the trooper opened up with his sidearm.

Shit. I didn't think this through. What if the bastard nukes my truck?

James ran around the other side of his vehicle and shot toward the shimmer. No new blasts of concentrated electricity followed, and several bright flashes signaled he was hitting something.

The bounty hunter barreled forward and dropkicked the empty space. His boots connected with something solid and a loud groan filled the air. A dent appeared in the Crown Victoria.

James pushed himself off the ground as soon as he landed and pummeled the air, his fists thudding against an invisible body. After the fifth new dent appeared, the shimmering air solidified to a bloodied and unconscious wizard, his wand still in his hand.

"*Fuck*, that's annoying." James tossed the wizard to the ground and returned to the F-350 for a quick inspection.

Relief flooded him. No bullet holes or magic-induced scorch marks.

Several sirens sang in the distance. Reinforcements.

James took a deep breath. "You okay?"

The cop nodded. "Yeah. *Fuck*. That's the first time I've had to deal with this kind of shit on the job. Pulled over a speeding gnome once, but the only magic he displayed was the magic of being a smug prick."

"Glad I could help."

The whole wizard incident ended up only costing James an hour's delay once the other cops arrived. The state trooper thanked him for his assistance and sent him on his way after the bounty hunter gave him an autograph.

The enemy had obviously upped their game, but James' only real worry was that they might damage his truck or hurt an innocent bystander. Even though it'd increase his travel time, he decided to move off I-5 at least part of the time to follow some of the less trafficked roads. According to his phone, it'd add a decent number of hours and have him in LA next evening instead of the afternoon.

Shouldn't be a big deal, and less chance of some random fifty-car pile-up once someone decides to drop a bomb on me.

Hours later, as he closed in on Eugene, Oregon and his next major barbeque stop, The Spice Vortex, the incident still lingered in his mind.

The people hunting him, whether a group or several groups, couldn't be dismissed. If the guy had managed a better impersonation of a cop, they might have been able to take him by surprise and blast his non-amulet-fused ass with lightning.

In every situation where he'd relied on the amulet he'd known he'd be facing danger, and the length of time he used it was limited. If he waited during his trip, someone might get a major shot off when he was vulnerable, but the idea of wearing the thing for an entire day of travel and dealing with its mind-whispers didn't sit well with him.

You know what? Fuck it. I've managed to get halfway into Oregon without using the amulet. I think I can get all the way back to LA without it.

He rubbed the amulet through his shirt, both comforted and disgusted by its presence.

Just because I might be an alien doesn't mean I have to go full-freak all the time. Probably don't appreciate barbeque wherever the fuck I'm from. Martian-style barbeque? Fuck that shit.

16

Fatigue had long since set, along with the sun, but James wanted to make it to a rest area close to Sacramento. Then it'd be just one more day of travel to get back to LA, and he wondered if it'd be as hectic. Or if it'd at least involve fewer attempts on his life.

In addition to the knife boys and the wizard patrol, James had been attacked by a half-dozen other assholes on his way through Oregon and northern California. Several others had been more creative, such as a man faking a car wreck and trying to steal his truck.

James' plan to avoid I-5 had worked to reduce the number of people around him, but there'd still been a few close calls in addition to the state trooper who'd almost gotten fried.

The bounty hunter glanced at the briefcase in the passenger seat, the cause of all his trouble.

Fucking assholes would probably just end up blowing themselves up if they got what they wanted.

James needed a little sleep, but first he had some prep work to do.

He pulled out his phone and dialed Peyton, wondering if the man was still awake.

"Ah, good evening, Mr. Brownstone. What can I do for you?"

"You found something out easy enough, but I'm wondering if you could put something out there just as easily?"

"What do you mean?"

"Do you know where I am right now?"

The researcher didn't answer for several seconds. "On your way back from Seattle, from what I've heard."

"Yeah, that's right. I need the people who are snooping around to think I'm heading to a certain place."

"What place?"

James grinned to himself. "The Black Sun in LA. Can you make sure people hear that?"

"Sure, for a fee. All that electricity isn't free."

The bounty hunter snorted. "Fine, I'll pay a thousand. This shit can't be as hard as research."

"You have a deal. I'll spread the word. Hope you survive whatever crazy shit you're doing."

"Thanks."

Peyton hung up and James smirked. Enjoying messing with scumbags wasn't a crime. Maybe a sin, but not a crime.

That little hint would take care of the end of his trip, but right now he needed to handle the immediate threat.

He glanced in his rearview mirror; there were still a few familiar cars behind him. If he hadn't been paying close attention he might have just thought they were going the same way, but the coincidence of them pulling off for gas at the same time and following him onto and off state highways had focused his attention.

The only question he couldn't answer was why they hadn't tried to attack or trick him yet.

These assholes are waiting for reinforcements. The question is where? Sacramento? Or are they just waiting for me to go to asleep?

His phone rang, cutting through the droning hum of the highway. Unknown number.

He answered it on speakerphone.

"What?" James barked.

"I presume I'm speaking with Mr. James Brownstone?" The voice was deep, masculine, and accented, but he couldn't quite place the accent.

"Yeah. Who the fuck is this?"

"Just think of me as a party interested in cutting you a deal."

James checked around to see if any of his tails were driving suspiciously, but they were all keeping their distance.

"What deal?"

"You're currently transporting an item of interest to me, and I'm willing to offer you a good reward if you'll turn it over me."

"I have no fucking clue what you're talking about."

The man let out a quiet laugh. "Here's the thing, Mr. Brownstone. I'm not some idiot gangster. I'm a man of means, and I've been tracking the crystal. I have grand plans for it. I haven't had my men attack because you're not someone I'm interested in angering. I understand why you've done what you've done in the past. Those Harriken disrespected you. I won't make that mistake. I have nothing but the utmost respect for you and your abilities."

"Those are some good instincts. You should stick with them."

"Exactly. So instead of angering you, I want to make you happy. I want to treat you as I would wish to be treated."

James laughed. "Leaving me the fuck alone would make me happy. Why not do that?"

"That's one possibility," the man agreed. "But I have another option. A way we can both benefit and be happy."

"And what's that?"

"A better offer than your current employer. I suspect it's Smite-Williams, but it doesn't matter. You see, I'm willing to pay two hundred and fifty million dollars for the artifact, and I know that old drunk doesn't have that kind of money to throw around."

James grunted. "Who are you, anyway?"

"That's something you don't need to know at this time."

"Well, I know you're one rich son of a bitch."

The man chuckled quietly. "Oriceran represents great business opportunities. I realized that early on, and have profited accordingly. In this case, you don't have to do anything but hand over something that's caused you nothing but distress."

James had always wondered if he had a price. Years of high-level bounties assured that even if he quit his job he'd never have to worry about going hungry, but he was still a hobo compared to a man who could throw around such huge sums of money.

Some people said everyone could be bought, and James had always half-believed that. Maybe that was true, but the money being offered wasn't high enough.

Guess we'll find out some other day if I can be bought.

James cleared his throat. "This kind of shit always makes me think about 1 Timothy 6:10."

"Excuse me?"

"The Bible. A lot of people get that one wrong all the time. They think it says, 'Money is the root of all evil.' It doesn't say that, though."

"Oh? I just might have to start going to church." Mr. Rich Dude snorted. "I'm glad to see you can be reasonable, Mr. Brownstone. I knew it was a good thing to contact you and explain my position."

"Nah, you don't get it. Yeah, it doesn't say *that*, but it does say 'Love of money is the root of all evil.' I love a lot of shit, including barbeque and my truck, but money, not so much. Just a means to an end."

"I'm offering a very great means," the man ground out, his voice tight. "More than you'll ever hope to gain, no matter how many scumbags you drag into the police."

"I can live with that."

A weary sigh followed over the phone. "Don't be a fool, Mr. Brownstone. With the money I'm offering you, you could move to some beautiful tropical paradise overlooking an ocean. You could leave that pathetic little garbage dump of a neighborhood behind, along with all those cockroaches."

James snorted. "You don't know me very well. I like my

neighborhood, and those people you're calling cockroaches are my friends. You want what I got? Come and take it, asshole." He hung up.

He eyed an exit sign. He was still far from the rest area, but the light traffic suggested this was a good place to have a showdown.

Wonder what Sun Tzu would say about this shit? Some sort of battlefield preparation shit, I bet. Maybe I should ask Trey later. Or, fuck...I could read the book.

The cars following him sped up. James took the exit, accelerating as well, and scanned for a good place to beat down a rich asshole's paid thugs.

There was an abandoned gas station up the road, complete with grass and weeds shooting through the cracked pavement. Perfect.

James whipped off the road and screeched to a halt next to the pumps. He grabbed an already prepped tactical harness from the back seat and finished slipping it on as five black sedans pulled off the road.

The bounty hunter exited his truck, .45 already in hand. Ten suited men with automatic rifles filed out of the cars, bathed in the bright light of the full moon. Two other men wore the same dark suits but held no obvious weapons.

Wonder what their deal is?

"Do you assholes really want to do this?" James shouted. "You know who I fucking am? *Do you?* How many dickwads do you think were in the Harriken headquarters in LA? How many in Tokyo? Huh?"

A few of them exchanged nervous glances.

"Our employer has instructed us that if you immediately surrender the item, you're not to be harmed," one of the men without a gun called. "You can leave, and his initial offer stands. If not, I'm afraid you die here, Mr. Brownstone."

James crept away from the F-350, taking the briefcase with him. He didn't want his truck to be turned into Swiss cheese again. He sprinted toward the side of the abandoned convenience store that had once connected to the gas station.

Muzzle flashes lit up the pump area and glass shattered the few remaining unbroken windows. James laid down a few shots of his own and one man fell with a groan.

The men continued their bursts of fire as they advanced in a rough line. James downed two more with quick shots.

He'd credit the men for discipline. A lot of lesser thugs would have broken and run the minute a couple of their guys dropped. They were already three men down and keeping up their fire.

The men broke into two groups, obviously intending to encircle the building.

James threw a frag grenade and sprinted around the corner.

"Grenade!" a man screamed.

The explosion roared in the night a second later. James didn't continue running around the building. Instead, he popped around the original corner to empty his magazine into several dazed thugs. The enemy force now was only six men strong.

Bullets whizzed by him as he retreated around the corner and rushed toward the rusty back door. He dropped the empty magazine and slammed in a new one.

The bounty hunter ripped the door off its hinges and

rushed inside as pairs of men turned the corner and sent a bullet storm his way. The bullets pinged and sparked against the metal door from the other side.

James threw another grenade toward the riflemen as he rushed toward the front of the abandoned convenience store. He charged the front door, shoulder-first. The worn hinges didn't stand a chance and the door flew out.

He cringed, but it missed his truck by a few inches.

Shit. Better be careful. Could have hurt something important.

James pointed his gun back and forth, looking for survivors. The two unarmed men walked around the corner with frowns on their faces. The bounty hunter fired twice at each but they didn't even twitch.

"Yeah, figured that," he muttered.

James holstered his pistol and threw a knife at one of the men, but it bounced off harmlessly.

The other man twitched and the bounty hunter grinned. He pulled out two more knives and threw one at the man's leg.

He snapped up his arm and cried out as the blade embedded itself in his leg. The next knife ended up in his head, and he fell to the ground, a pool of blood forming beneath him.

"This is why I hate magic. It makes no fucking sense that a knife works, but a gun doesn't. What's up with that?"

The remaining man shrugged. He'd been the one who spoke before. "It all makes sense for the particular magic. Why would a man be protected except for his heel? It makes sense once you know the way he became protected." He cracked his knuckles. "It's always good to see someone who lives up to their reputation, Mr. Brownstone. When you ran, I worried that I wouldn't even get to play."

"What's your deal, asshole?"

"That would be telling."

James put down the briefcase and raised his fists. "I just killed all your friends, including Magic Boy Number Two over there. You want to keep breathing, you can get in a car and drive off. Otherwise, I hope your will is fucking up to date."

"Ah, there's a thin line between arrogance and confidence, Mr. Brownstone."

The bounty hunter narrowed his eyes, wondering if he should bond with the amulet. The process didn't take a huge amount of time, but it also wasn't instant.

Nah. Waited too long.

James charged the man, throwing a series of quick jabs. The man blocked with a few soft grunts but didn't stumble back, which proved he was much stronger than the average man.

The man slammed a fist into James' stomach and the bounty hunter hissed as pain shot through his abdomen. It was a nice solid blow, but was a step below the strength of the hits from someone like King Pyro.

So he's tough, but not super-strong. I can deal with that.

An exchange of blows followed. James blocked his opponent's hits, but his own didn't seem to be doing much other than making the man twitch.

The man jumped back and pulled a knife from a sheath under his jacket. He tossed it from hand to hand with a wicked grin on his face. "Maybe the best offense really *is* a good defense."

The enemy swiped a few times with his blade but didn't land a hit. James waited until he overextended, then grabbed the man's arm and yanked backward. The man grimaced, but his bones didn't break. His knife clattered against the asphalt and the blade glowed red for a split second.

James smashed his shoulder into his opponent. The man stumbled backward and let out a low growl and the bounty hunter took his chance, snatching the knife from the ground and shoving it into the man's chest.

The other man's eyes widened. "No…" He backed up, pain and fear etched on his face. His skin darkened and shifted, and after a few seconds his pale smooth skin had been replaced by a rough gray texture.

"What the fuck are you?" James let go of the knife and pushed the man back with his foot. "I'd say some shit about I expected more from you, but I don't even know who the fuck you are."

The now-rigid suited statue hit the ground and broke into several pieces.

"Yeah, that was different." James reached down to grab the knife, only to find a molten puddle. "Yeah, of course. What a fucking rip-off."

He retrieved the briefcase, got into his truck, and roared off.

17

James headed into the parking lot of an abandoned electronics store. Weathering had left the original name unreadable, but it had ended with "City."

He pulled out his phone and checked his texts and emails. Trey had been a busy little hunter, racking up more than a few bounties in recent days. The reputation of the Brownstone Agency was growing with each capture. Once they brought Royce on, agency action would explode.

Trey's success without James holding his hand also proved the agency was a good idea and could sustain itself without him running things on a day-to-day basis.

The bounty hunter chuckled. He wondered if there would be any low-level bounties left in Los Angeles within a year.

We're gonna fucking scare every asshole out of this city. Then, I don't know, go clean up San Francisco or some shit.

A familiar black Porsche pulled in right next to his F-350. His four-day odyssey was finally coming to an end.

In truth, he was a little disappointed. It'd been a long time since he'd hit up so many new barbeque places. Even in Los Angeles, he'd gotten too comfortable with going to the same places.

They weren't *bad* places, but the quest for ultimate barbeque understanding required him to go outside of his comfort zone.

Going to Jessie Rae's again and again was a different matter. Maybe the God Sauce itself was the ultimate barbeque flavor, hence the name. He'd need to make another trip there soon for research purposes.

Addie Endo opened her door and stepped out of her car with a faint smile on her face.

The bounty hunter rolled down his window and held out his finger. The courier retrieved a DNA scanner from her purse and did a quick check.

"You know that's not enough, big boy. Got to be sure. I need the passphrase."

"Come on. It's been a busy last few days."

Addie rolled her eyes. "And I know you didn't forget it. You know the deal. DNA plus passphrase or I walk."

James gritted his teeth.

"A young woman got married last noon,
Her boyfriend she kissed, and gave a swoon,
Her mother laughed and said, 'You're in luck,
He's a stunning good fuck.
For I've had him myself down in the saloon."

Addie snort-laughed. "Yeah, that's it. Things like this make me love this job."

"You have other people using dirty limericks as passphrases?"

"Nope, you're the first." The courier reached through the window of her Porsche to pull out a briefcase. "Can't believe this shit worked." She handed it to James.

"It wouldn't have without the artifacts. One sent a signature like the crystal, and the one I loaned you suppressed it just enough. If I hadn't been bait, they would have figured it out. All about being the noisiest deer in the woods."

Addie whistled. "Can't believe you'd basically throw up a flare that said, 'Attack me, assholes!' when you didn't even have anything worth guarding. You've got balls of steel, Mr. Brownstone."

James grunted. "It worked, didn't it?"

The courier gave him a little salute. "That it did, big boy. That it did. It was fun. Hope you enjoyed being the bait." She winked. "Until next time."

The courier slid into her Porsche and pulled away with a wave.

James stared at the briefcase containing the Atlantean crystal. He hadn't run into any serious trouble by his standards, and he'd managed to sample a lot of great barbeque up and down the West Coast. All in all, a good trip. Almost a vacation.

The Professor reappeared from the back room of the Leanan Sídhe, the briefcase with the crystal and the other with the magic signature artifact gone. He retook his seat across from James.

What the fuck kind of set-up do they have here that the

Professor feels comfortable storing something like that in the back?

"That went well." The Professor picked up his beer and took a drink. Unlike the last time they had met, he was already red-faced. Not a single line of tension marred his face. "*Very* well. Even better than I had anticipated."

"Does the owner of this place know you've basically got a magical nuclear bomb in their back room?" James glanced toward the door and shook his head.

"Aye, he does know, trust me. I've made arrangements. No one will be able to track it here, and I'll be moving it again soon enough."

"One trusting guy." James shook his head. "So what's the plan? Gonna bury it next to the Ark of Covenant while top men examine it?"

"Aye, something exactly like that."

James glanced back at the back room again. "Kind of makes me wonder how many things like that are out there."

"Too many, lad. Trust me, you'd rather not know." The Professor shrugged and sipped his beer.

James nodded. "Hey, when I was out on the road, some douchebag offered me two hundred and fifty million to turn it over."

"Were you tempted?"

"Not really. What the fuck would I even *do* with two hundred and fifty million dollars?"

The Professor chuckled. "Many men would have turned it over for far less."

"Guess it's a good thing I'm not most men. Just thought you should know that some really rich asshole is interested in it. He even mentioned he thought you might be the one collecting it."

"Thanks, James, but I already knew that. You can't be in this business as long as I have without figuring out who is interested in the same sort of things." A mischievous smile appeared on the Professor's face. "But enough of that. I'm more interested in something else."

"What?"

The Professor leaned forward, an all-too gleeful look in his eyes. "I trust that Ms. Endo made you use the passphrases?"

James grunted. "Yeah, she did. Was she just fucking with me?"

"No, lad, not at all. For all her playful manner and appearance, she takes her job deadly seriously. If you hadn't given the passphrases she would have left. If you had attempted to force the matter, she would have tried to kill you. No, those were the passphrases *I* insisted on. The more you use dirty limericks, the more comfortable you'll become with them. I was trying to help you and help with security at the same time."

"You mean you were trying to make me think about your dumbass contest," James muttered.

"You do owe me participation, James." The Professor sighed. "That's the problem with you, lad. If you feel like you're going to embarrass yourself, you will. This is why I'm never embarrassed."

"Because you have no fucking sense of shame?"

"Exactly. Shame is just power over you that you give to others. I've taken it all back. It's a freedom you'd do well to seek."

"I'll keep that in mind during the next Bard of Filth competition."

James' phone chimed with a text and he pulled it out, surprised to see that the message was from Shay. He'd lost track of time with his focus on the Professor's job.

Hey. I'm leaving Japan in the morning. Prepare for a trip to South America. There's something I need to check out down there, and it might help to have a sidekick.

"Huh. Shay's coming back, and I guess we're going to South America?" James shrugged, wondering if he should be demanding more details or objecting to the trip. "Fuck. This is why I'll never be a tomb raider; all the fucking plane rides."

The Professor slapped a hand on the table. "This is divine providence, lad."

"Huh? What the fuck are you talking about?"

"There is something I need from South America—the Lost Map of Piri Reis. If you're already going down there, what's a quick jaunt to southern Chile? It won't be a hard trip. I already pretty much know where it is, and I was planning to have Miz Carson go down there anyway."

James grunted. "Depending on where we're going, that's not a quick jaunt, Professor. Besides, why don't you ask her directly?"

"Because I think she'll be more inclined to do it if you ask and are with her, even with all the zeroes after the three I'm willing to pay. I'll send you an email with the details, and you just pass it along. If she says no, that's fine."

"And what if *I* say no?"

The Professor smirked. "I'll just note, lad, that it'll be a lot of time to spend with the lovely Miz Carson. Your choice."

James thought that over. He still wasn't certain if spending more time or less time with Shay would be the best strategy, but some quality time kicking ass and collecting artifacts together wouldn't be so bad. "Okay, I'll at least pass it along."

"Excellent."

James' phone chimed again. "Huh. Another… Wait. This isn't from Shay. It's from that prick Tyler." He burst out laughing. "Guess my little hint worked."

Fuck you, Brownstone. I'm going to find a way to pay you back. Fuck you. Fuck you. Fuck you.

Tyler finished the text with ten poop emojis and ten middle-finger emojis and the flag of Malta for some reason that escaped him.

He dropped his phone on the bar. "That fucking son of a bitch. He sent these assholes here on purpose."

Screams filled the room as people ran for the front door and the emergency exit.

A green energy ball blasted across the room, exploding in a shower of green and blue across the wall.

"That was just fucking painted!"

The target of the energy blast, a man with a pistol, ran across the room firing away at the witch who tried to fry him. "Brownstone's mine, bitch!"

The bullets near the witch melted into vapor in green fire. The remaining rounds added new holes to the recently renovated bar. Several bottles shattered behind the bartender.

"My fucking booze!" Tyler yelled, ducking glass shards. "This is the Black Sun and this place is fucking neutral, assholes. Brownstone isn't here!"

A third man, the asshole who had initiated the whole thing, lay on the ground, moaning from the huge burn on his chest.

Several of the people running for the exit suddenly leapt to either side.

Oh, fuck! What now?

Two pairs of helmeted black-armor-clad AET officers rushed in from either exit, their weapons at the ready and their red goggles down.

"AET!" shouted one of the officers. "Stand the fuck down!"

Tyler recognized the magnified voice of Lieutenant Hall through the helmet speaker.

Gun Boy spun and opened up on her, but his bullets just bounced off her armor with embarrassing pings. She raised her rifle and put a single round into the man's leg.

The witch raised her wand, but a blue pulse from another officer's AET stun rifle sent her to the ground, twitching. Whatever spell she was using to block the bullets didn't work on energy.

Tyler stood and started picking glass off his shirt, satisfied and more than a little surprised. When he'd called 911 to report three criminals looking for Brownstone he'd not expected such a swift response.

Guess the lieutenant really does like this place.

The cops hurried over to the downed suspects and

cuffed them. Lieutenant Hall grabbed the witch's wand and set it on the bar. "Someone get me a containment bag."

One of the other cops ran toward the front door. The lieutenant pulled Gun Boy up by his collar.

"Why the hell would you come to this bar for Brownstone? Not one fucking person here wants him around, and that includes me, the cop." She pointed to a Yakuza sitting in the corner, sipping some sake and looking bored. "A criminal and him." She pointed to Tyler. "The fucking owner of this joint!"

The lieutenant kneed the wounded man in the head, knocking him out. She pulled off her helmet. "I fucking hate morons."

Tyler surveyed the damage. The quick action of the AET meant the showdown had produced only minor cosmetic damage. He was pissed, but it was manageable.

Several patrons filtered back in, eyeing the downed suspects with satisfaction. The Yakuza in the corner, who hadn't moved, raised his cup of sake and gave Lieutenant Hall a polite nod.

The bartender poured four drinks and set them on the bar. "For you and your men, Lieutenant. I know it's not your favorite, but they blew up the bottles of what you like."

Hall rolled her eyes and kicked Gun Boy again. "Asshole," she growled. "Whatever. Let me drink this shit before I have to go do paperwork."

James chuckled. "Fuck you, Brownstone. I'm going to find a way to pay you back. Fuck you. Fuck you. Fuck you."

"Such eloquence that man has!" The Professor laughed. "And look at you. You're so good with people, James. Such a naturally radiant personality."

"He'll live. Fucker profited off gambling on my life. Just wanted to remind him that he doesn't hold *all* the cards." James stretched, giving a loud yawn. "Well, shit. It's been a fun last few days, but I think I'm gonna go get some rest. Especially if I have to get ready to go to fucking South America on a damned plane."

"Thanks for your help. Be well, lad."

James stood and headed toward the door. A busty blonde in a thin scrap of cloth that could only charitably be called a dress winked at him, leaning forward to show off her tits.

He ignored her as he made his way toward the door and the blonde frowned.

The Professor laughed and called. "Tell Shay she has some competition."

James rolled his eyes. "No fucking way. I might be the first one killed."

18

James stepped into the main room of Warehouse Five, the final door locking behind him. Without Shay opening the way he'd have a hard time getting into the place. Given she stored artifacts in the place, the high level of security made sense.

So she'll let me into a place with valuable artifacts, but she still won't let me near her precious books in Warehouse Four? That's some bullshit.

Then again, if I had kept my cookbooks in a place like this I wouldn't have lost them to that rocket launcher motherfucker.

The dark-haired beauty waited for James by the wall, her arms crossed and a smile on her face.

James nodded, surprised by how his heart rate increased after not seeing her for so many days. "Hey, Shay."

"Brownstone." She pushed away from the wall. "What's this about the Professor having a job for me?"

"The Lost Map of Piri Reis, whatever that is. He says it's

in Chile, and he already has the location. He said he was gonna ask you to grab it soon anyway, but since we're heading to South America he wanted me to push you to do it now."

Shay snickered. "Yeah, like you can get me to do anything I don't want to."

James shrugged. "Just said I'd ask. He's offering three million for it."

"Three million?" The tomb raider furrowed her brow and gave a curt nod. "Yeah, that should work. We're going to Argentina anyway, so we actually will be close."

"And why are we doing that? Going to Argentina? You never told me."

Shay pointed to James' chest. "You wearing your Whispering Amulet of Doom?"

James winced. "Don't call it that."

"Why? Because it bothers you, or because you believe that's what it is? You think you're gonna piss it off and it's gonna go on strike or some shit?"

James grunted. "Just saying, and no. I was using it for a job, but I've got it in my warehouse now."

She laughed. "Yeah, your storage unit is totally the same thing as a warehouse." She gestured around. "Maybe you should store it here."

"Nah, I'm good with my warehouse."

"Your shit, your choice. Anyway, I wasn't in Japan on a tomb raid. I was there doing some research on the glyphs on your amulet. Lots of artifacts there that might be potentially linked to aliens. Figured it'd be better to inspect some of them up close. You never know what people might hide about artifacts, magical or otherwise.

Some of the information I found pointed me toward Argentina."

"Why didn't you tell me that?" James frowned. "I thought you were on a tomb raid."

"Because you get like a mopey goth teen girl when it comes to that amulet. I didn't want you brooding about it when I was gone."

"I don't fucking brood."

"Said every goth teen ever." Shay snickered. "I'm gonna need you to bring it along. The amulet. For all we know, it could interface with something and Marlon Brando could pop out to explain why he sent you away from Krypton to begin with."

"Fine." James shrugged. "It's not a big deal. I'm gonna be cautious with the thing until we know more, but I'm not scared of it or anything. I want to know the truth as much as you."

"Good, then it'll be easy. I've basically got the location down, so it's not like we're gonna be wandering all over Argentina."

"A nice in and out?"

"Yeah, I'd like a nice in and out sooner than later."

James stared at her, confused by what she meant.

Shay sauntered to him and patted him on the shoulder. "Bend over. You have something on your mouth."

James blinked, but complied.

The woman wiped his mouth, then launched a devastating sneak attack in the form of a quick kiss.

The bounty hunter stared at her, wide-eyed.

What the fuck just happened?

Shay winked. "Didn't want to taste barbeque sauce." She

gave a little wave and wandered toward some rows of shelves on the other side of the room. "And I figured I'd start moving shit along. There's taking things slow, and then there's the speed of molasses."

James stared at her, unsure of how to process or handle what had happened. Bounty hunting was easy—you tracked down a bounty and you kicked their ass—but dealing with women was the most complicated shit he'd ever encountered. And he sensed dealing with Shay would be even more complicated than dealing with most women.

He couldn't deny his heart warmed when he was around Shay, but he also didn't even know what the fuck he *should* be feeling. Sure, he'd read about relationships and all that bullshit, but everybody had their own spin, and he didn't know which was right. Or normal. As if he could ever hope to experience something normal.

Most people didn't help deliver dangerous Atlantean power crystals. Most people didn't stab men with magic knives and watch as they turned into statues.

If Shay was right, James wasn't even human. Even if they were biologically similar, how could he be sure his brain functioned the same way? He might not be capable of understanding human relationships.

For all his understanding of the minds of bounties, the simplest social interactions sometimes eluded him. That was how he made it decades without any real friends other than the Professor until recent months, and he could never be sure how much Smite-Williams actually liked him.

James grunted.

Fuck. Having a life is fucking complicated.

An hour later, James motioned around the empty living room of his now-completed house. "Obviously, I need furniture and shit, but it's all ready to go. Bill sent me an email yesterday saying everything's complete, including the saferoom hatches."

Shay nodded. "It's nice, Brownstone. This is your chance to loosen up a little bit and not be so anal. A few scratches and piles here and there from day one will help cure you of your neatness addiction."

"Keeping things organized helps keep things simple."

"Remember, the first part of getting help is admitting you have a problem." Shay nodded firmly.

James ignored the jab and led Shay into a bedroom down the hall. "This is gonna be Alison's room. Tried to make sure she has a lot of space, but every time I mention that she says she doesn't need it."

"I don't give a shit if she's blind. She's a teen girl. She'll fill the space." The tomb raider held up a hand. "And I'm gonna decorate and furnish this one."

"Why you?"

"Because If you do it it'll probably be in meat colors or some shit like that. Even if Alison can't see the decoration, she doesn't deserve to be subjected to Barbeque Bachelor style."

James snorted and opened the closet door. He pointed to the carpet. "There's a hidden hatch that leads to a basement safe room."

"Nice. *Very* nice. I didn't know you were doing that."

Shay knelt and felt around the floor. "I guess once you know where it is you can see it easier, but what about her?"

"I've got a runes witch who'll be helping me out with that. She'll produce some shit that normal people won't be able to see but Alison will." James headed toward the hallway. "Kind of strange to have it come all together like this. It's even better than my old house, and..."

He stopped and looked over his shoulder. Shay still stood in the room, looking around with a smile on her face.

"You've done good, Brownstone," Shay told him, her voice almost a whisper. "You've done good. You make a hell of a dad."

Shit. Should I say anything?

"Uh, what time are we leaving tomorrow?" James blurted. "For Argentina?"

Shay blinked and shook her head as if refocusing herself. "I booked us tickets for a morning flight. Supersonic, so I can minimize your whining about flying. Still a six-hour flight, though." She frowned. "You know what? Send me the Professor's info. I think it'll be better to hit that up first. I'll reschedule the flight and do some quick background research tonight."

"You want to go straight into a tomb raid?"

"Yeah." Shay shrugged. "No point waiting around. I'll pack, do my research, and meet you at the airport tomorrow morning. You bring what you need. Not worried about a lot of crap in Argentina, but if the Professor is passing a job my way, Chile's gonna get a little messy. So, you know, *accessorize*."

"You mean bring lots of ammo and grenades?"

"Yeah. Always got to wear the outfit appropriate for the event."

James grinned. "Hey, it's the Southern Hemisphere."

"Yeah, so?"

"It's not almost summer there. It'll be cold. All the more reason for me to bring a coat."

Shay scrubbed a hand over her face. "You're just wearing those coats to fuck with me, aren't you?"

"A man can have more than *one* hobby."

Widowmaker smiled to herself as the red Fiat Spider pulled away, driven by the woman known as Shay.

Thank you, Professor. I would have never suspected Brownstone had such a weakness.

The Drow had planned to destroy Brownstone anyway, but harvesting him after deceiving him in the form of his lover would be so much more potent and satisfying.

She'd waited for some time already. A delay of a day or two more so she could end the life of James Brownstone in such a delicious manner was too great an opportunity to pass up.

The Drow slashed her hand through the air and a dark nimbus surrounded the car for a moment, then vanished. Her magic marked the Fiat with a rune invisible to mere humans like Shay. Now she could track the woman home at her leisure.

"Thank you, James Brownstone, for being difficult to find. You've presented me this wonderful opportunity."

Widowmaker licked her lips.

19

The next day, the noon sun was high in the cloudless sky as Widowmaker parked her Ferrari down the street from a two-story brownstone, the home of Brownstone's lover. She'd tracked Shay's vehicle to the home and was more than happy to kill the woman if she got in her way.

You picked the wrong lover, Shay. And your lover picked the wrong princess to hide.

The Drow took no pleasure in slaying a female, but using the woman's shape would help her uncover the missing princess and help her finish off Brownstone once her interrogation was complete.

After Widowmaker's attempts to get Brownstone's attention had failed in the Leanan Sídhe, she had accepted that she would need to make stronger efforts to seduce him.

Most humans were weak, but the Detroit police and the bounty hunter proved that a few had spines. The strong will of a few humans wasn't enough to impress her, but it provided for a more interesting hunt.

Widowmaker took a deep breath and called to her magic. The cost of her next trick would force her into an earlier harvest, but she couldn't risk discovery.

A dark miasma surrounded her and her body slowly faded, becoming insubstantial. After several seconds, only her shadow remained.

The flat shadowy form writhed under the door of the Ferrari and swam across the ground until it reached Shay's front door. Widowmaker slipped inside the home.

Pure darkness blasted from the shadow and the sphere of energy enveloped the house before disappearing. Whatever feeble defenses Shay had set up would be disabled for long enough for the Drow to complete her business.

This is the power of magic, humans. Your technology will always be weaker.

Widowmaker returned to her solid form and listened for her prey. Only the tick of a wall clock kept the silence at bay.

Gone are you, Shay? It doesn't matter. I can kill you whenever I like.

The Drow didn't care to explore the human's home, other than to find some useful physical token. She'd only seen her from afar, and that wouldn't be sufficient to get a good likeness. An actual link to her body would grant better insight, something necessary to deceive her lover.

Widowmaker stepped into a bathroom and smiled as her gaze landed on a brush. She pulled a single dark strand of hair off it.

"Perfect," she whispered to herself.

The Drow held the hair between her thumb and forefinger and stared into the mirror as she shimmered into a clone of Shay. She took a few deep breaths as she reached deeper into the link between the hair and the woman. Not a true connection to her soul, but enough.

I understand now, Shay. You're a tomb raider? Don't make me laugh. You're a scrounging parasite who feasts upon the artifacts of superior beings.

Widowmaker tossed the hair on the bathroom counter and headed upstairs to Shay's bedroom. She threw open her closet and looked through the hanging clothes.

"I have the look. I have the smell. I have what he wants. I just have to find the princess, and then I will have James Brownstone…for lunch or an after-dinner snack."

James and Shay made their way through the rough earthen tunnel, their headlamps cutting through the darkness and their footsteps echoing.

The bounty hunter ducked to avoid hitting his head. "These tunnels are too fucking small."

"Guess the average Inca was shorter than the average Brownstone." Shay chuckled. "Plus, who the fuck knows? These *Pucará de Cerro La Muralla* tunnels might not have been something that the average Incan even knew about. You saw the shit I had to do to reveal the hidden stairs, right?"

"What's some foreign map doing underneath an Incan fortress in a place where people can't even find it? You never explained that."

"You didn't ask. You're not always the most curious guy, Brownstone."

James grunted. "I figured you'd fill me in when I needed to know."

Shay smirked. "The basic deal is that even though many of his maps have disappeared or been destroyed by people trying to cover up the truth, Piri Reis produced maps that were way too accurate for his time. As in, some of that shit people didn't have down until centuries later, and in some cases, there were things that modern maps don't show at all. Lost continents and shit like that."

"Huh."

"Yep. There are a few journal fragments that discuss him using some sort of 'collective dream' to help him map, based on dealing with people in certain key points." Shay shrugged. "Always thought most of it was bullshit, but the Professor dug deeper. A lot of people have tried to explain why certain places had much better cartographical knowledge than they should have, and some have even gone so far as to suggest there was like a guild or a cult or whatever the fuck you want to call it dedicated to understanding the true map of the world. Some sort of metaphor for understanding God or something. Hard to say with people back in the day."

"I don't get it. So you're saying it's his map, but someone else here made it after talking to him in a dream?"

Shay nodded. "Yeah, basically. That was just how they rolled—at least Piri Reis and some of the people he was in contact with. Not a lot of information left about his group."

"If all that shit was happening, why did anyone bother

to send out explorers? Seems like a waste of time if they already knew everything that was out there."

"Same reason as always—control. Can't have these magical bastards communicating in dreams and sharing information." Shay ran a finger across her throat. "Lot more people killed for simple shit back then than most people realize. Not like they could just upload it to the internet. Pretty easy to suppress information, and a lot of these guys didn't even realize they were doing shit that would get them in trouble."

"Yeah, guess so."

The tunnel widened into a vast stone chamber with three more equally spaced exits. A pile of rocks all but blocked one of the exits, and the partially caved-in ceiling provided their original source.

Piles of white stones littered the floor. Focusing his light on a white stone, James grunted. No, not rocks.

"Shit. That's a lot of bones."

Shay frowned and swept her light across the chamber. "Yeah. That's a shit-load. Too many, especially considering how hard it is to get in here."

"The place above used to be a fortress. Got to stick dead soldiers somewhere. Maybe there's a shaft or something that we can't see, or it got filled in?"

The tomb raider shook her head. "I'd still expect fewer intact bones. These might be fresher."

"Fresher? How fresh is 'fresher?'"

"Who the fuck knows? I could be wrong. It's pretty dry in here. Could be months. Could be decades. Could be centuries old, and I'm worrying about nothing." Shay shrugged. "Or it could be a skeleton army ready to rise.

Never know on a tomb raid anymore. I don't tell you half the fucked-up shit I see."

James shrugged. "In Detroit, I just decapitated a guy who could hop bodies."

"We have some fucked-up jobs."

They both laughed.

Once they calmed down, Shay pointed to an elaborate geometric pattern carved above one of the exits. "That's where we need to go."

The pair made their way down another narrow tunnel that opened into an even larger chamber. Small jagged holes covered the walls and ceiling but the stone floor was unmarked, even if the bones made it hard to see.

A stone obelisk rose from the center of the room, with complex geometric patterns covering it from top to bottom. They spun in a circular pattern that directed the observer to a golden plate inside a hole in the center of the monument. Etched silver lines covered the plate.

James moved closer to the plaque, bones crunching underneath his boots. He narrowed his eyes. "Wait a second."

Shay rushed past him with a grin on her face. "Yep. It's exactly what you think. I love a good artifact discovery."

Now closer to the plaque, James could clearly make out the continent on the gold and silver map. A few large land masses that didn't exist on current maps decorated the plate.

How many years had passed since the map had been accurate? Hundreds? Thousands? It was hard to know, given all the knowledge that had been suppressed.

"Fucking nice," Shay whispered. "Okay, just one last

little bit and we can grab this shit and get out of here. It'll take a minute or two to complete the ritual to remove it from the obelisk, though."

Something chittered in the distance.

James looked around the room, his headlamp cutting from wall to wall. "You hear that?"

"I'd like to say no, but that would be bullshit," Shay muttered under her breath. "I guess if this shit was gonna be easy, the Professor wouldn't have needed me to do it. Do your 'kill 'em all and let God sort them 'em out' thing while I get the map."

The tomb raider pulled out a dried herb from a pouch on her belt, crushed it, and rubbed it all over her palms.

Scratching joined the chittering.

James unholstered his gun. This shit wasn't going to end well. This was why he preferred bounties. He didn't like being the one hunted.

Shay placed her hands on either side of the map and chanted something in a language James didn't know, not that managing that was hard. A bright yellow glow surrounded the plate and illuminated the chamber.

Fuzzy, jointed legs covered half the ceiling, connected to spiders with glistening fangs. James didn't give a shit about spiders normally, but these bastards were the size of pit bulls. It was going to need a little more than a boot heel to take them out.

Shay kept chanting and the glow grew brighter.

A spider leapt from above and James planted a .45 bullet in its head, splattering it into pieces. The body crashed to the ground, scattering the bones that covered it. More of the eight-legged monsters emerged from the holes and their scurrying and chittering echoed in the chamber.

James emptied his clip into the nearest spiders, but for every one he sent to spider hell two more poured out of holes. He reloaded with a grunt.

"Damn it, this isn't a fight—it's fucking pest control. I should have brought a can of Raid."

Shay stopped chanting and the glow faded. The tomb raider took a deep breath and snatched the plate from the obelisk. She shoved it into her backpack.

"Let's get the fuck out of here!"

They sprinted toward the tunnel. The thuds of spiders hitting the ground echoed in the chamber, but a writhing, crawling mass of fangs and legs continued to follow them like a wave of death, eager to add their bones to the collection.

James and Shay's bullets brought down the trailing giant arachnids with ease, but the creatures showed no fear and reinforcements ran right over their dead. The humans wouldn't be able to outrun the swarm forever.

"Fuck." The bounty hunter reloaded. "Run ahead of me. I've got an idea."

Shay kept up her pace as James slowed. "I hope this isn't a dumbass idea, Brownstone."

"It probably is, but it's better than getting eaten by giant spiders."

"That's a low fucking bar to clear, but I'll take it."

They hit the earlier chamber, Shay in the lead. James reached into his backpack and pulled out a C4 charge.

"Guess we didn't need to dig with this shit, but it can still be useful." He keyed in a delayed timer and threw it with full strength toward a crack in the ceiling before sprinting into the entrance tunnel.

Hope I judged that right or it's gonna be a sad fucking day for me.

The swarm grew closer.

"Four, three, two, one..."

The tunnels shook with the force of the explosion and a grinding rumble continued to shake them after. Screeches and shrieks echoed through the tunnel and clouds of dust billowed from the chamber behind them.

James sped after Shay, his heart pounding. The shaking and rumbling continued, and portions of the tunnel behind them collapsed.

Both kept running until they arrived at the stone stairs leading them back to the main ruins.

Shay leaned over, panting. Sweat covering her forehead. "Way to close the back door." She winked. "But just so you know, I don't like back-door action."

"Huh? I got those things off us, didn't I?"

The tomb raider rolled her eyes. "Never mind; too lowbrow for you, I guess. Or maybe some shit in the past didn't go the way you liked."

James wiped at the dust coating him. "Is this something I need to look up? And what *about* my past?"

Shay held up a hand. "You know what, never mind. I don't want to know. If you had a bunch of women in your past, I'd have to go kill them one by one."

The bounty hunter stared at her, more confused than when they'd started the conversation.

"Let's get the hell out of here. At least tomorrow

shouldn't involve…" Shay gestured down the stairs. "Any of that sort of shit."

"Okay," James rumbled. He still didn't understand what Shay had been going on about before, but even for the Scourge of Harriken, sometimes discretion was the better part of valor.

20

Widowmaker walked into the Leanan Sídhe, enjoying the looks men shot her way. So many weddings rings, so many targets—but she wasn't there for a harvest. At least, not yet.

Shay had a nice appearance. The Drow wasn't sure if she preferred it to some of her other recent disguises, but it would be a useful weapon even if she weren't hunting Brownstone.

Still, even a quality weapon should be tested before its use in battle, and that was why she'd returned to the pub. The Professor had acted as if he'd smelled through her disguise before, so it'd be good chance to see how thoroughly her new appearance would fool someone who knew Shay well.

The man wasn't anywhere in the room, so the Drow headed to the bar.

The bartender smiled. "Hey, Shay. What can I get for you?"

Widowmaker smiled back. "I was looking for the Professor, but I don't see him anywhere. Is he in the bathroom or something?"

"Nope, he's not here at all. He left a couple of hours ago. I can give him a message for you if he comes back in."

The Drow shook her head. "No, it's all right. It wasn't anything important. I'll just throw him a text and catch up with him later. Hey, you seen Brownstone around?"

"Nope. Him neither. Sorry."

Widowmaker gave him a little wave and headed toward the door, smiling to herself.

Not a full test, perhaps, but still a successful outing.

Her heart swelled with confidence. The plan would work. Soon the location of the princess and James Brownstone's life would both be hers.

The way Shay had built up the ruins in Argentina, James had expected some vast temple filled with hidden chambers; something similar to what they'd wandered through in Chile the day before. Instead, what he got were a pile of broken rocks and a few cracked pillars.

Previous expeditions had pushed back the trees and bushes, so at least they didn't have to dig anything up.

Archaeology struck James as what the Devil might force him to do as a punishment. Sitting around carefully digging while worrying about breaking some lost unique thing sounded painful.

Shay grinned. "Whip it out, Brownstone."

James blinked. "Huh?"

She nodded toward a pillar. "Your amulet, dumbass."

He pulled out the amulet. "What about it?"

Shay pointed to the top of the pillar. Glyphs circled it. "Look familiar?"

James didn't even need to check his amulet to know the answer to that. This was the first time in his life he'd seen anything that matched the symbols on his amulet.

"Son of a bitch.! I know you've been talking about them, but seeing them… Shit, it's weird."

"So here's the deal. I've traced these symbols all over the world. Here, Japan, Egypt, Iceland, and Australia, and those are just the ones I've been to so far. I think people have been looking at them the wrong way, since the few people who are aware of them have assumed they have something to do with Oriceran."

"What do they mean, beyond being associated with sky gods?"

"That's where things get interesting." Shay grinned. "There are mostly the same symbols, but they have different patterns in the different locations. It's taken me a while to figure out why that is, and that's the big key to the mystery."

James stared at her, waiting for her to elaborate.

Shay lifted her phone and snapped a picture of the symbols on the pillar. "I collected all the data from the different locations and tried to figure out if there were any associations between the symbols and something about the location. I kept running into dead ends, and nothing made sense."

"But you figured it out?"

"Yeah, the Japan trip finally helped the pieces of the

puzzles slide into place." Shay took a deep breath. "Look, it's not anything about the places. It is the locations themselves. Using algorithms to process seasonal variations along with the longitude and latitude of the different places, and putting that together with the symbols, I think I found out what they are trying to tell people."

James grunted. "All that shit sounds complicated."

Shay pointed to the sky. "You're damned right it is. From what I can tell, these symbols are kind of an astronomical arrow. I think they point to the star system you're from. The fact that some of them are on your amulet prove your connection, not just that it's some other random alien planet."

"Shit, really?" James lifted the amulet and stared at the glyphs. "Where the hell am I from, then?"

Shay shrugged. "That I can't be sure of that yet. The more places I find the more refined things get, but I'm not an astronomer and we're still talking a really general direction. Not only that, it went against my first theory."

"Which was?"

"I figured it had to be in the star system Zeta Reticuli."

"Why?" James moved toward the pillar to get a closer look at the glyphs. "I'm guessing this shit wouldn't spell out anything modern-sounding, and even if it did, it's not like the ancients would have called it that."

Shay nodded. "Yeah. You see, before everyone started assigning all past weirdness with Oriceran, there were a lot of reports of alien abductions associated with gray aliens, and some people claimed they came from Zeta Reticuli." She shook her head. "Once I got going, though, the arrow wasn't indicating that system at all." She pointed to the sky again. "It's somewhere in that general vicinity, but I still need to collect more information before I can narrow it down. It's a big fucking galaxy, you know, and like I said, I'm a tomb raider, not an astronomer. But I'm getting closer, Brownstone. A lot closer."

James stared at the sky. Night had yet to fall. Any of the nighttime visitors hanging in the firmament might mark his true home, a planet lost to his normally-perfect memory.

"I wonder if it matters." The bounty hunter shook his head.

"What do you mean?" Shay furrowed her brow.

"Look, I appreciate what you're doing, but I grew up on Earth. It's not like I can go back to Amulet Land or wherever. I don't even know how the fuck I *got* to Earth." James rubbed his fingers over the amulet. "Huh. Listen to me… Guess I'm through fucking second-guessing this. I don't know if I believed I was an alien before, but I do now." He shrugged. "But I can only be me—James Brownstone, bounty hunter."

"I'm about the last person to be giving advice to people about their past, but I think you need closure or some shit, and if I can help provide that I will. Maybe you can't go back. Maybe the planet got blown up by some space dragon, but it'll feel good to know."

James grunted. "Yeah, probably would. Thanks for figuring this shit out for me."

"No problem, and now the next step will be unlocking your amulet."

"Huh? What unlocking? I didn't know it was locked."

James turned the amulet over as if he could find some obvious mechanism he'd missed before.

Shay pointed to the amulet. "It's got the symbols that I've found all over, but it also has some I *haven't* found elsewhere. I think the inscription is the key to unlocking its true power."

"It's pretty damn powerful as is."

"Yeah, but I'm thinking you could do more with it."

James slipped the amulet back underneath his shirt, the cool metal of the separation plate touching his chest. "Wonder if that's a good idea?"

"Can't know until you try, right? You want to come to terms with your past? That's what you're gonna need to do. I'll keep digging into things and trying to figure it out for you. That's the least I can do."

James nodded. "And what about you?"

Shay looked confused. "What about me?"

"What about coming to terms with *your* past?" The bounty hunter shrugged.

The tomb raider snorted. "I did that already, remember? I got fed up with the killing and realized it was a fucked-up life. Did the whole fake-my-death thing and all that. Burned my fucking house down."

"But you're also still running from someone. You can't move forward when assholes are gunning for you. I should know. I didn't choose to burn down my house, a fucker with a rocket launcher did."

"So what? We've all got baggage. I'm dealing with mine, just like you're dealing with yours. Mine doesn't involve alien amulets, though."

James shook his head. "I run *toward* people, not from.

The Harriken kept fucking with me, so I ended them. Now I don't have to worry about their shit ever again."

"What are you getting at?"

"Just saying I couldn't have built a new house I would feel comfortable with Alison living in if I hadn't taken care of the Harriken. So, like I said, what about you?"

Shay narrowed her eyes, discomfort spreading across her face. She looked away and didn't speak for a long while. "The Nuevo Gulf Cartel. They are the ones who wanted me dead, but it was more an excuse. It's not like I'm running from them in particular. They make it harder for me, since they'd come after me if they knew I was still alive."

"Aren't you tired of running? Tired of looking over your shoulder?"

Shay shrugged. "It doesn't hurt to be careful, Brownstone. Even if the cartel disappeared tomorrow, I still have a lot of shit and people from my past I need to worry about. Fuck, I've already made a couple of enemies in my new career."

"I'm careful, but I also know at the end of the day I don't have to worry about the Harriken." James rubbed his chin. "Not saying you have to deal with this shit alone. I can help. You *know* I can help. I might know fuck-all about ancient history and artifacts, but beating the shit out of people? I've practically got a degree in that."

"It's not your problem." Shay gritted her teeth. "It's *my* problem."

James pointed to his chest. "I'm making it my fucking problem. You didn't have to help me with the Harriken, but you did. It wasn't your fucking problem. You made it your problem."

"You don't get it, Brownstone." Shay shook her head. "These Nuevo guys? They own half of Mexico. I doubt you'll find many bounties on them because they own the system. There's no money here. This will just be a lot of ass-kicking with no payout."

James marched over to Shay until he was so close she could feel his breath. "I killed a lot of Harriken before I started getting bounty money for it. Some shit is more important than money. Your fucking *life* is more important than money."

Shay's eyes widened. "You're serious, aren't you?"

"Yeah, but it's your choice. Let's end the cartel. Who gives a shit if it solves all your problems? It'll take care of at least some of them."

"Fuck it, you're right. Might as well give them a real reason to hate me."

The next day, James leaned against the wall of Warehouse Three and waited for Shay to finish gathering her gear.

Shay peered down at a selection of handguns. "You sure about this, Brownstone? This shit is gonna get bloody."

"When does shit *not* get bloody when I'm around?"

"Fair enough. Just saying we'll be killing even more people than in Tokyo, and we killed a lot of people in Tokyo."

"I'll go confess to Father McCartney later. We're doing the world a favor by wiping those assholes out. They are helping strangle a country. They kill innocent people in a way even the Harriken would spit at. Fuck them. The sooner they're dead, the better."

Shay grinned. "Not saying I disagree, just wanted to make sure you knew what you were signing on for." She picked up a pearl-handled pistol and aimed down its sights. "Might as well try this baby out. I don't think I've broken this in. You got everything you need?"

James tapped the amulet underneath his shirt. "You have all the ammo I need here, and you also have the nice goodies like grenades and explosives so I don't even need to go back to my place. This is like Walmart for ass-kicking supplies."

"Great. Enjoy your shopping, but I'll be right back. Gonna go check on something." Shay put down the gun and headed around a corner toward more racks of weapons and equipment.

James pulled out his phone. Despite his big speech about not needing bounties, it wouldn't hurt to check. He checked for an organizational bounty on the cartel and couldn't find one. A quick cross-reference with the top ten leading figures in the cartel pulled up a few bounties, but the amount was pathetic. He'd never seen such powerful criminals with such low bounties.

Shay is right. They've manipulated this shit. This amount isn't enough to get two flour tortillas warmed up with sand between them. I think the guys Trey is bringing in right now are worth more than half these guys combined.

The few bounties on cartel members were all from small private donations, with no government or large companies involved. It was like everyone was afraid of looking like they would dare oppose the cartel, and there were just a few villagers here and there with nothing left to lose.

Even worse, it was like the bastards were begging Shay and James to come and kill them. Shay's checks on the dark web had revealed that the higher-ups of the cartel were having a huge meeting at a private resort—some sort of celebration of their recent successes.

James and Shay couldn't take out everyone in an organization with thousands of direct and indirect members, but the bounty hunter was sure Sun Tzu'd had something to say about cutting off the head of a dragon and the body dying.

The cartel was already under siege from various enemies, both criminal and law enforcement. All it needed was a little push, and the piranhas would feast on the dead body.

Yeah, fuckers. See how you like being the hunted.

Shay's information suggested there would be over five hundred cartel members at the resort. It'd be a tough fight, and the amulet would get a work-out. If it craved blood, it'd get more than its fair share.

James grunted. He should take more explosives. Sometimes you just needed to blow up a building or three.

Peyton emerged around the corner with a frown on his face.

"Problem, Peyton?"

The younger man looked around for a moment. "I'm always monitoring stuff in case people are looking for me or Shay." He shrugged.

"Yeah, and?"

"I was, uh, poking around in the LAPD system, and I found out that AET is looking for Shay."

James' jaw tightened. "Why would AET want Shay? How the hell do they even know who she is?"

"They got a partial long-distance image from a drone from that airport fight when you guys took down that assassin. From what I can tell, the AET reached out and the FBI sent them some information back linking the image to…well, Shay. They don't know her real name, but they know she was a hitman on the East Coast and think she's dead—that sort of thing." Peyton sucked in a breath. "Shit, what should we do? If they get serious, it'll be hard for her to hide. Too many drones and cameras in this city."

James scrubbed a hand over his face. "Keep this to yourself for now."

"Huh? You serious? Shay needs to know."

"You heard me. Shay needs to concentrate on this cartel shit. This AET crap is my fault because they have such a hard-on for taking me down. Let me handle it. I'll work something out."

Peyton sighed. "You sure? This seems like something I should tell her."

"I'll solve the problem. For now, Shay needs to stay focused. Besides, if I can take down the Harriken and help take down a cartel, I can get a few cops off Shay's ass."

21

"Hello?" a deep-voiced man answered in Spanish. "This is the Hotel Azul."

"Do you speak English?" James rumbled. He didn't want his fumbling Spanish to mess up the message he needed to deliver.

"Yes, sir. How may I help you?"

"Tell the head of the cartel that James Brownstone and a friend are coming for him."

He hung up.

James watched through binoculars from his comfortable hilltop perch as hundreds of cartel enforcers and guards spread out along the fences surrounding the main resort complex. Frightened resort staff poured through the gate into waiting buses and cars.

"Looks like they are clearing out everyone but the cartel

douchebags. I don't think they want anyone tripping over them when the bullets start flying."

Shay glanced at the distant resort. "That shit works well for us. That means we can go forward with our plan."

"Yeah. Can probably hit them in less than an hour. Maybe half an hour, at the rate they are booking it out of there."

James might be ruthless when it came to wasting cartel assholes or gangsters, but he wasn't about to lay out some poor maid because she just happened to be changing the sheets in some dickwad's room. Even if the cartel owned the place, that didn't mean that every random employee was a piece of shit.

He'd just concentrate on killing the tattooed motherfuckers with guns now setting up around the area.

Shay hauled a large metal case out of the back of the trailer connected to their first rental vehicle, a large truck. "You really think it was a better plan to threaten them ahead of time?" She laid the case down. "Whatever happened to the element of surprise? Not like I told marks I was coming for them. We could have kept it clear enough even without using any of surprise and just shot anyone with a gun."

"Surprise is overrated. Fuck, it wasn't like the Harriken didn't know I was coming the last time. Didn't do them a bit of good." James lowered his binoculars. "We want these assholes on edge. They'll make more mistakes that way." He grinned. "You might have more experience as a killer, but I have more experience taking down large groups of fuckwads at once."

Shay rolled her eyes. "For fuck's sake, don't get too

cocky, Brownstone." She opened the case and started assembling the sniper rifle inside. "I've taken out plenty of groups of people. Hell, I was with you on two of your Harriken raids, and when it comes to clever plans and timing that rely on something other than just punching or shooting anything that moves, I have way more experience."

James shrugged. "Punching or shooting works most of the time."

"But not all the time. Sometimes gunning down a lot of people requires finesse." She winked. "And a woman's touch."

James moved over to the dozen drones parked to the side of the trailer and inspected the explosives strapped to each. Even with his bounty-hunting reputation, bringing in such large amounts of *boom* toys would have proven difficult, so they'd relied on Shay's smuggling skills.

He chuckled at the ease with which she'd moved all the materials into the country. So much for Customs.

"I bet this shit's gonna be real easy."

Shay looked up. "You think so? I'm not saying it'll be hard, but maybe they'll give us a halfway-decent fight."

"Once shit starts blowing up they'll freak." James grunted. "These assholes don't have any real discipline. They are just a bunch of thugs used to scaring everyone. Now it's our turn to fucking scare *them*."

After all, unlike the Brownstone Agency, they didn't have a Marine DI training them. Royce would whip the men into shape.

James furrowed his brow. Everything was almost ready.

"And you're sure you managed to get everything set up last night?"

"Yeah. Unlike you, I'm sneaky and good with disguises. No one suspected a thing." Shay nodded toward the resort. "They don't empty any of the main trash bins until noon, so all my surprises should still be there, and since they didn't evacuate the place before your call, I'm guessing no one found anything and all the other ones I slipped around the resort are still there."

"Don't know how many we'll get with the surprises, but it'll at least confuse them."

Shay chuckled. "This shit's gonna set a record for both of us. Lots and lots of guys in there. Guess they were worried about someone attacking them even before your little threatening call." She finished setting up the sniper rifle and placed it atop its bipod. "It's annoying as shit, though."

"What is?"

"Those assholes are so cocky they don't even have any surveillance drones up. I feel kind of insulted on some level."

"You want them to have better security? You'd prefer if they had a row of assholes in exoskeletons and weird-ass Oriceran monsters down there?"

Shay shrugged. "I just don't like their arrogance."

"I bet they figure, with that many guys it doesn't matter."

"See, this just proves why it's important not to get a big head and push too hard."

James hauled an RPG and a crate of ammo out to place next to the sniper rifle. "What do you mean?" He returned to the trailer and started stuffing magazines into his tactical harness.

"They got too big, even with other guys fucking with them. Thought they were untouchable, even when I was slitting the throats of some of their guys." Shay stood and double-checked her knives. "When you push too hard, eventually someone's gonna push back."

"Sure some Harriken were saying that shit about me." James gave her a feral grin.

"Well, never push someone you know is stronger." Shay nodded toward their second vehicle, a Toyota 4Runner. "Did you get the maximum insurance again?"

"Yeah, but I don't know how much of it'll they'll honor if I bring it back full of bullet holes. And that's assuming it even survives."

Shay laughed. "You know what you need to do? You need to buy a whole shitload of junker cars for situations like this. Why do you think I have a lot of those ugly-ass vans and shit in the Warehouse Three Annex? Sometimes you just need a piece of shit to ram through a gate."

James shook his head. "My life used to be fucking simple. This whole attacking-assholes'-bases thing didn't used to be something I did every other week." He shrugged and lifted the binoculars again. "Looks like the last bus pulled away. Huh. Wait. That's fucking annoying."

"What?"

"Six trucks with heavy machine guns just rolled in. They look military, but it doesn't look like soldiers driving them. Looks like cartel douches, from what I can see."

"Probably took them from a local unit or bribed one." Shay shrugged. "As long as they aren't rolling in with tanks the plan should still be good." She pointed at his chest. "Can the Whispering Amulet of Doom protect you from a heavy machine gun?"

James snorted. "Don't know. Let's just kill those fuckers before I have to find out." He grabbed a few more grenades from the trailer. "I'll need about twenty minutes to get into position, but I think we should get this shit started."

Shay fished a large antenna-laden military-grade jammer out of the back of the truck. "We need to find some sort of magical walkie-talkie, so if we have to do this shit in the future we can still talk to each other."

"That sounds complicated."

Shay laughed. "Is there anything about this plan that *isn't* complicated?"

"Just saying, adding magic makes shit even *more* complicated. This plan just involves blowing people up or shooting them. It's about as fucking simple as things get."

"Anyway, I'll flip this baby on once the first round of fun begins, so if you're gonna contact me do it before then. You comfortable with the timing?"

James shrugged. "Not like it won't be obvious when the party starts."

"Glad to hear you're onboard." Shay clapped. "Okay, let's get ready to decapitate ourselves a cartel."

James flattened himself behind a large bright-yellow truck with obscenely huge tires in the parking lot. Shay and Peyton's intel indicated the ranking cartel men would all be on the top level of the resort. By the time shit got serious and they realized the danger it'd be too late for them to flee, but cutting off their escape routes would ensure their doom.

The bounty hunter sent a text to the local police department with only one sentence in both English and Spanish.

Brownstone is fighting the Nuevo Gulf Cartel. Stay away.

Even if the local authorities didn't want to take on the cartel, he doubted they wanted to die to protect them. The enemy already knew he was coming, so it didn't matter if a corrupt cop tipped off the cartel.

"Everyone finish getting into position!" a man shouted in Spanish.

I'll just note, lad, that it'll be a lot of time to spend with the lovely Miz Carson.

The bounty hunter smirked at the memory. He didn't doubt the Professor'd had this exact sort of thing in mind.

It's more fun than hanging out at the beach, that's for sure. Plus, this doubles as a public service. I'm being all efficient and shit with my time.

"What the fuck is that in the sky?" another man shouted.

The whirring hum of drones filled the air.

Time to blow some shit up.

The amulet whispered in the back of James' mind, restrained, quiet, and measured.

James readied a frag grenade and took a few deep breaths. A hundred feet up a squadron of drones flew in formation, then six broke off from their fellows to dive toward the trucks. The machine guns roared to life, but the cartel gunners realized their mistake too late.

Three explosions engulfed trucks, blasting them off the ground and showering the area with metal and plastic. The gunners on the other three managed to clip the closing drones but fared no better as falling explosives hit their vehicles.

The deadly threat of the six machine guns had been reduced to burning bodies, rubber, and metal.

Sucks to be you guys. Bet you thought you were badasses up there with the big guns, huh?

A series of massive explosions ripped through the resort's buildings. Men screamed, and clouds of fire, dirt, and cement shot into the sky. The defenders had barely finished processing what happened when another series of explosions rocked the area.

James launched himself from his cover and threw grenades like fastballs at clusters of cartel enforcers and foot soldiers. Still recovering from the earlier blasts, they didn't even have time to open their mouths before they collapsed in a mass of blood.

The remaining explosives drones slammed into several buildings in the resort and the loud report of the .50 caliber sniper rifle followed, mixing with the crackle of the fires all over the area.

The whispers in James' mind remained quiet and controlled. Easy to ignore.

James jogged toward the front gate at a leisurely pace. He blasted away with the .45 and finished off a dozen stunned men before they could manage more than a few shots at him.

Surviving men poured out of burning buildings and rushed toward James. They unloaded on him with their rifles and pistols, their bullets stinging but not piercing his flesh. He'd need a new coat when this was all over.

Like a tattooed Angel of Death, the bounty hunter moved with grim determination, firing a gun until empty and then reloading. His victims groaned and cried out as they fell, one after another.

How long have you bastards bled this country? How many lives have you fucked up, assholes?

Shay's sniper rifle continued to crack in the distance. James had no idea if he could take a sniper rifle round to the head, but the explosives and the tomb raider's overwatch would handle that in the first phase of the plan.

Thick clouds of smoke darkened the skies.

Three trucks screeched to a halt in the debris-covered parking lot. Men armed with AKs filled the back. James ignored them and continued advancing on the main hotel building.

An RPG slammed into the first truck, and a few seconds later another destroyed the second. Half of the men managed to make it off the third before Shay's next attack enveloped them in hellfire.

If she's using the RPG, all the snipers are taken care of.

James picked up the pace as he headed toward the building at the center of the resort. Killing enforcers bled the cartel, but this was supposed to be a decapitation attack. They needed to kill someone more important than random Señor Juan *Sicario*.

They might have gotten lucky with some of their explosives, but they lacked the power to bring down the buildings—which meant they'd still need to confirm their kills.

The bounty hunter closed on the hotel lobby. RPG warheads continued to hiss from afar and slam into buildings around the resort, creating a torrent of glass, wood, and metal raining down.

"She should save some of that shit," James muttered. "Might have another truck we need to blow up."

A man with an ax spun from behind a cement pillar and screamed, and James dropped him with a shot between the eyes. Another popped up and fired a burst from a submachine gun.

James grunted and shot the man twice in the chest. A few cuts marred his chest, but most of his wounds could be handled with a Band-Aid. Not bad, considering that the coordinated attack had already killed hundreds of cartel men.

Shit. I should try to keep it to one shot per guy. Gonna have to start borrowing weapons again before I'm done.

The amulet continued to whisper in the back of his mind, but there was no urgency to the tone or texture. Maybe it was satisfied, or it didn't feel there was any danger.

"You like this shit, huh?"

A line of twenty enforcers stood inside the double glass doors that opened into the hotel lobby. James leapt to the side as they opened with automatic rifles. Shards of glass shot through the air and sliced his clothes, but not his skin.

Better not press my luck. At least they've made it easy to clear them out.

James returned the favor with a couple of grenades. The

screams cut out seconds later, and the bounty hunter spun back toward the now-shattered doorway. A few survivors moaned softly, bleeding out from their wounds.

He needed the ammo, so he left them to die.

Glass crunched under James' boots and fire alarms wailed as he jogged toward the stairwell. Between the drone explosives, the planted explosives, and the RPG rounds, the fire escapes and electrical power were neutralized. If the higher-ups wanted to escape, they'd have to hoof it down the stairs.

Okay, Shay. Hurry and get here for the next part of the plan.

22

The stairwell door flew open and cartel enforcers poured out of it, blasting at the bounty hunter. James calmly put round after round into their heads. He ignored the sting of the bullets and the whispers of his amulet.

He could be dodging more. Hell, he probably should. The amulet protected him, but it wasn't like it kept him from *all* damage. He wanted to test it, though, to see how far his alien ass-kicking power could go when he just didn't give a fuck about being careful.

Unlock it. That's what Shay had said. He'd barely made use of some of its power already. The armor was simple and easy to understand. What else could it do besides enhancing his telekinesis?

He waved his left hand and two enforcers' guns dropped to the ground. He shot the unarmed men.

Would it be easier to use it more?

More men surged out of the stairwell, and James had to

credit their bravery. The survivors kept charging and firing at him until nobody was left alive. The heavy footsteps and shouts of more men echoed from above.

The deafening alarm mixed with the thundering gunshots drowned out the screams of the dying men.

The building groaned, and the acrid stench of smoke filled the air.

Fuck. Why do this the hard way when I can do it the easy way? Fuck the plan. I've got a better one.

The raid wasn't about style. It was about killing lots and lots of motherfuckers, and the building was on fire in several places.

No firefighters were going to roll into a war zone, especially when they'd been warned who was responsible for it.

James rushed outside, picked up the ax from the man he'd killed earlier, and used it to jam the stairwell door. With all the fires eating the building and the stairwell blocked, none of the cartel's men left inside would survive.

"Yeah, that should do it." The bounty hunter dusted his hands together and nodded to himself, satisfied.

The new tactic also saved James the trouble of hoofing it up multiple flights of stairs in a burning building that might collapse halfway through his shooting spree. This way, he'd just need to wait outside in case any cartel members made it through the door. More boring, but also more ammo-efficient.

A vehicle screeched to a stop outside and James rushed out of the lobby, his gun at the ready. He waited for an explosion that never came. Shay must have been out of rounds.

But the new arrival wasn't a truck filled with cartel

reinforcements. It was Shay behind the wheel of the 4Runner.

She stuck her head out the window and honked the horn. "Get your ass in here, Brownstone."

James sprinted to the passenger door and hopped inside the vehicle.

Shay peeled out before the bounty hunter had even closed the door. "Those fuckers played us, and they almost got away with that shit." She slammed a fist on the steering wheel. "I guess we should have planned on them having no balls."

"Huh? What are you talking about?" He nodded toward the window. "We've been dropping the fucking boom here. I've got the stairwell sealed and was just going wait and clean up. Why are we leaving early?"

"We've been killing a lot of guys, but not the top guys. The fucking pussies are running. I spotted four trucks booking out the back. It's the fucking cartel leadership."

James grunted. "You sure they aren't just carrying some enforcers who decided they didn't want to die?"

It might be brave to stand and fight after hundreds of men died around you, but it could also be considered stupid. James wouldn't blame any cartel enforcer who broke and ran. If the Harriken had learned that lesson earlier they might still exist.

Shay shook her head. "Nope, it's the big boys. I spotted the head of the cartel in the passenger seat of one of the trucks and one of the top lieutenants in another."

"Damn."

"Yeah. I nailed one with the RPG, but there are still three left. I think the assholes must have been spooked by your threat call. They distracted us with the peons while they ran. Shit, I don't even know if their own men knew about the plan."

"Yeah, I don't think they would have stood and fought like that if they thought the big guys were running."

Shay frowned. "Maybe we shouldn't have had you call."

"Guess there is such a thing as *too* badass a reputation." James shrugged.

"I'm guessing that's why we didn't run into any magical assholes. I know they have a few nasty witches and wizards working for them. I was half-worried they were going to zap my ass with a fireball while I was sniping."

"Any of those witches and wizards immune to C4?"

"Probably not."

"Problem solved, then. They probably bit the big one during the explosions. If they hadn't, they would have put a fight."

Shay chuckled. "On that note, look in the back."

The RPG and a box of warheads sat in the back, but there were only four rounds left. Shay'd had all the fun.

The 4Runner roared through the carnage zone. Bodies lay all over, and hungry fires now consumed half the area. The flames would finish what James and Shay started.

Shay whipped between the gates. The RPG rolled in the seat as she took a hard turn. The vehicle now straightened, she pressed the accelerator to the floor, her eyes narrowed.

"Not letting those fuckers get away."

They barreled down the road. Three trucks glinted in the distance.

James grabbed the RPG from the back and loaded it, an

awkward experience in the cramped quarters of the vehicle.

"We need to get them before they hit the city. We start dropping lead and grenades there, the military's gonna show up."

"Yeah, I'm sure it'd make for great TV to have the Mexican military in some huge gun battle with James Brownstone."

The bounty hunter frowned.

Shay let out a dark chuckle. "Don't worry. You just get ready to shoot. I'll get us close to them and we'll finish this shit."

A couple of minutes ticked away as the 4Runner closed on the three trucks. Shay gritted her teeth and kept both hands on the wheel. One small mistake and she might lose control of the vehicle. They probably wouldn't get another chance to take down the Nuevo Gulf Cartel like this.

The trucks drew closer, and James smiled to himself. He didn't get to play with things like RPGs and rocket launchers nearly enough. They were fun.

James rolled down the window and leaned out. The air whipped past him as he aimed the shaking weapon. The bumpy road denied him a clear shot, but an upcoming curve in the road gave him a better opportunity.

"Fuck it." He pulled the trigger.

The round launched, flying not toward the back vehicle, but the front of the convoy. The projectile slammed into the truck. The explosion knocked it onto its side.

Shay hit the brakes, the tires of the 4Runner squealing in complaint.

The driver of the second truck tried to make a hard left

to avoid a collision but ended up flipping the vehicle for his trouble. The third truck slammed on its brakes and managed to avoid slamming into either of the other two.

It was still a fatal mistake, since it gave James time to reload and send an RPG into the vehicle. He repeated the process, then grabbed the last round. With a satisfying hiss, it zoomed away and blasted the wreckage a few feet into the air.

"Just making sure."

Shay snickered.

James dropped the RPG into the back.

They watched the burning wreckage for a moment, waiting for any enemies to crawl out and return fire. James half-expected some statue bastard in a suit to pop up and start mocking him for thinking he could win with a few explosive warheads.

Shay and James hopped out of the 4Runner, their pistols at the ready, but the weapons proved unnecessary. There wasn't a single man left alive. Hell, there wasn't a single man left *recognizable*.

The tomb raider laughed. "I don't know if that counts as overkill or underkill."

"As long as they're dead, it doesn't matter." James shrugged. "You know, the bastards might have had a better chance if they hadn't run. Made it easier for us in the end."

"Huh. So, we've done it. We've killed the leadership of the Nuevo Gulf Cartel and their top muscle. Fuck."

"Yeah. The cartel won't last long now. Maybe the survivors can start a new gang with the survivors of the Harriken."

Shay stared at one of the burning trucks. "Who knows?

I heard the Harriken were founded by a survivor of a Yakuza family that got wiped out by some magic chick."

James grunted. "Then they should have fucking learned their lesson, just like these assholes."

"Thank you for your business, sir." The rental agent smiled from behind the counter.

The 4Runner didn't even have a chip in the paint. The rental company had won their gamble as far as the insurance went.

For James, the whole raid had been far cheaper than his last few jaunts, considering they'd mostly used Shay's explosives.

He grinned to himself as he stepped away from the counter and passed through the thick crowds toward Shay, who was leaning against a wall with her arms crossed. There was a pensive expression on her face.

He wasn't looking forward to getting on another plane again so soon, but Shay had never acted like she cared before. Something else must have been wrong. He expected her to be happier after taking down the people who had forced her to fake her own death.

The bounty hunter eyed her, not yet willing to face a woman he didn't always understand. "Ready to head back to LA?"

"No."

"No?"

Shay nodded. "You're gonna head back to LA, but I need to make a side trip to Europe."

"Europe? Another tomb raid?"

"Nope." Shay peeled off the wall, and the pair joined the dense flow of people in the airport. "I didn't mention it earlier, but Peyton sent me a text. It turns out that not everyone important was at the resort." She frowned. "Two of the top guys are still on the loose."

"Then let's go find them and finish what we started. Not like I've got better shit to do than moving stuff into my house."

"They aren't in Mexico." Shay shrugged. "They are in Europe." She stopped and nodded toward the long lines snaking in front of the ticket counters. "I need to book a flight and head over there. If I don't finish off everyone in the top leadership the cartel could reorganize and survive, and that'd make what we did entertaining but pointless."

James grunted. "Make it a flight for two."

"And hear you bitch the entire time over because your happy ass has to be on a long flight? No, thanks. It's a lot longer flight from Mexico to Europe than Mexico to LA. No, I've got this. I can handle a couple of assholes." She grinned. "Tracking down and dealing with people this way, especially in exotic foreign countries—that shit is definitely much more in my wheelhouse than yours."

"I can still help."

"Nope. If anything, you'll get in my way. You don't have contacts in foreign countries, Brownstone. The Japanese shit only worked out because of who you were going after. If you go all...*Brownstone* somewhere else, it might just end up with you arrested."

James grunted. "You don't know that."

Shay placed a hand on his shoulder. "Look, thanks for

your help during the big show, but it's better this way. Closure and all that shit. You need to get back to LA and start getting your house set up before someone blows it up again."

"They better fucking not," the bounty hunter growled.

Shay winked. "I think most people have figured out why that would be a dumbass mistake at this point, but better safe than sorry." She stepped back and lowered her hand. "You should get going. Thank you for giving me my life back. Still not sure if I want it, but at least now I have the choice."

The tomb raider walked away and joined the Lufthansa line.

James continued toward Security. Shay was right. She could handle a few assholes, especially douches who were now trying to hide like roaches after the destruction the pair had delivered to their cartel.

If he wanted to help her, the best thing he could do was clean up the AET mess before she returned.

Guess I still have some shit to do.

23

The next evening James stepped into the Leanan Sídhe, acid gurgling in his stomach. The Professor had texted him, asking him to stop by and offer a few sample limericks as proof of his commitment to paying his debt.

James had hoped that getting the map might distract the Professor, but the man was obsessed with his damned limericks.

The bounty hunter wanted to tell the man to fuck off, but he did owe him for his help. He still didn't understand all the dirty limerick shit or its appeal. Cursing he got, but his brain just didn't want to put together a dirty limerick. He also didn't get why they were so funny.

Every single one of the limericks the Professor had told him was about as funny as a Harriken with a death wish.

The bartender waved to James as he passed by the bar.

"What?" he rumbled.

"Did Shay ever get a hold of you?"

James stared at the other man. "Huh? What are you talking about? She's out of town right now."

"No, no. I meant a few days back. She was here looking for you and the Professor. It seemed kind of important, even though she said it wasn't."

"She did," James lied. "Thanks, though."

"No problem, Brownstone." The bartender nodded toward the Professor's booth. "Be careful. He's had a lot to drink."

"When has he *not* had a lot to drink?"

The bartender laughed. "Good point."

James trudged toward the Professor, thinking about what the bartender had just told him. A few days ago Shay was with James, so how the hell could the woman be in two places at once?

She might have found some sort of artifact that let her do that sort of thing on one of her tomb-raider jobs, but if she'd had access to that kind of magic she would have bragged about it. For that matter, if she wanted to talk to him she would have just called or texted him, not played weird games involving asking around for him at the pub.

The answer was obvious. Someone was impersonating Shay.

James shook his head. First AET, and now an impersonator. James had a lot of shit to clean up for Shay before she got back from Europe.

Neither of us has a simple life, but if we kill enough assholes, maybe we can manage one yet.

The Professor was sipping some beer when James arrived, rosy-cheeked as normal.

"Sit, sit, lad. I'm eager to hear what you've come up with."

"I haven't had a lot of time to work on this shit."

"Yes, I've heard. You were busy blowing up cartels. But who cares? They are limericks, not novels." The Professor chuckled. "I need to hear what you have. Another Bard of Filth competition is coming up soon, and I want to make sure you'll put on a good show."

"We really have to do this now?"

The Professor nodded.

"Whatever." James leaned forward and cleared his throat.

"There was a man from Nantucket.
He really liked his bucket.
Some guys came by with pie,
Which they threw into the sky,
And he said, 'Oh, whatever, fuck it."

The Professor sighed and shook his head. "It's a limerick, but it's not a dirty limerick, James."

"How is it not a dirty limerick? I said 'fuck it.'"

"No, no, no. It's not just about a few curse words. It's about *sex*, James. Bawdy humor. Didn't you get that from the passphrases? They were supposed to help you understand the true nature of a proper dirty limerick."

James shrugged. "Still not quite getting it."

The Professor gulped down some more beer. "Do you have another one ready, at least?"

"Yeah. I got another one. I think you'll like it better."

"Excellent, lad." The Professor clapped once. "Let's hear it."

"There was an old man at the zoo,

*He really liked to smell poo,
A monkey came near,
And he yelled get clear,
But the smell was still true."*

A disgusted mask descended over the Professor's face. "Ah, lad, that's just terrible. Awful. *Awful!* I'm embarrassed for you. That's like something a schoolboy would come up with. It's fine if you're seven, but you're a grown man."

James looked away. "It's a fucking limerick that involves monkey shit. It rhymes and has the right order and all that. It's exactly what you wanted."

The Professor waved his hand. "No, this isn't happening. Not yet. You're not close to ready. If I let you go up there and offer those limericks, you'll embarrass us both. You'll defile everything the Bard of Filth competition stands for." He grimaced. "I won't be able to show my face in this place."

"I'll defile something with 'filth' in its name?" James grunted.

"Aye, you would. I guess there's no choice. There is no way I'm allowing you to embarrass yourself that badly, lad. I'm going to give you a little while longer to figure out what you're doing. Here, it's time for some more training with the master."

James grunted. He wasn't sure if he should be relieved or insulted.

A couple of hours later the drunken, filthy Professor stumbled out of the pub. James didn't feel like going home. His mind was trying to work through the appeal of bullshit like ribald cadences and dirty limericks.

He sat in the back by himself. At least he understood the appeal of Irish Stout.

"Hey, big boy."

James looked up from his beer and blinked. Shay stood in front of him in a red slip dress and heels.

He shook his head. "Wait, how are you back already?"

"Why wouldn't I be back already, James?" She smiled warmly and sat in the chair next to him. "It's hard being away from you."

"Huh? Really?"

Shay nodded. "Oh, yeah." She ran a finger up his chest. "It's hard when I'm not around my big, strong man."

Though his breath reeked of alcohol, Shay's only scent was a floral perfume he remembered her wearing before. Not only that, he'd seen her drunk before, and she'd never acted close to this.

"Are you feeling all right?"

The dark-haired beauty batted her eyelashes. "I'm feeling better now that I'm around you, James."

The bounty hunter narrowed his eyes. "What did you call me?"

Shay laughed. "How many beers have you had? I called you by your name. Would you prefer I call you something else?"

James frowned. "Sorry, you're right. The Professor's been training me, and it involved a lot of beers. Give me a sec. I've gotta take a leak." He stood. "I'll be right back."

"And I'll be waiting for you," Shay cooed.

James pushed into the hallway leading to the bathroom

and entered. He didn't know what the fuck was going on, but he did know that whoever was sitting at that booth wasn't Shay. Not even fucking close.

Even if the bartender hadn't mentioned a Shay showing up and looking for him, the behavior of the cooing woman at his table would have tipped him off.

James frowned. The Professor had also warned him about a suspicious beautiful woman. He must be dealing with someone who could change their appearance with magic.

"Who the fuck is she?" After a few seconds of thinking, he chuckled. "Doesn't fucking matter. This works out great."

James pulled out his phone and dialed Peyton.

"Hey, are you calling to make me richer?" the researcher answered.

James glanced at the bottom of the stalls to make sure he was alone. "Shay's still in Europe, right?"

"Yep. Why? Worried?"

"Nah. I just found a solution to the AET shit."

"I'm listening."

"There's a woman sitting in the Leanan Sídhe right now who looks like Shay."

"They say everyone has a twin. Guess you have a type, huh, Brownstone?"

The bounty hunter grunted. "She's a fucking clone. She's wearing one of Shay's dresses and some of her perfume. She's flirting with me like she's never seen a man before. And she's being too nice and calling me James."

"Okay, that's…suspicious and not very Shay."

"Yeah. If AET wants Shay so badly, they can fucking

have her twin instead. I don't know who this bitch is, but she's probably not gonna take me out for barbeque, so I figure we get *her* barbequed instead."

Peyton laughed. "Damn, you're ruthless. What's the plan?"

"Do your computer shit and send an anonymous tip to AET that the killer from NY will be at Lincoln Park in an hour."

"You want AET to go after some strange woman in the middle of a public park?"

"They're cops, they'll clear that shit out. That's why I'm giving them an hour."

Peyton whistled. "You really think this will work?"

"I think AET wants a scalp, so I'm giving them one. Can you do it? And how much will it cost?"

"This is for Shay, so it's on the house. You think you can lure this woman to the park without trouble?"

James grunted. "Yeah. She's practically drooling on me."

Peyton gasped. "I've got the perfect idea, and she'll totally fall for it if she's flirting with you and trying to be Shay."

"Okay. I'm listening."

Lieutenant Hall almost giggled with glee as she finished strapping on her armor.

"Make sure we bring the deflectors," she shouted.

Sergeant Weber eyed her. "Are you sure? Those are pretty expensive."

"I fucking know how much they cost. Brownstone can

clear entire buildings. That means he has access to magic, and that means the killer bitch with him has access to magic. We're bringing the damned deflectors."

Weber nodded and jogged to the other side of the armory.

The lieutenant grinned. It was her birthday and Christmas all rolled up into one. Once they took down Brownstone's floozy they'd make her roll on the bounty hunter, and then it was off to an ultramax for him.

I wish I could wave at Sergeant Mack on my way out. Your boy is going down.

After ten more minutes of Fake Shay's painful flirting, James figured it was time to move. If she wanted to try something in the car, he'd do what he needed to. Otherwise, he had a delivery to make to the cops.

"We should go somewhere. There's something I want to show you."

Fake Shay licked her lips. "I agree. We should go somewhere and exchange fluids."

"Sure, whatever." James stood. "You have a car here?"

"Yeah, I do, but I'll just ride with you."

James shook his head. "And risk someone stealing your nice car? Fuck that. Just follow my truck. It's not that far. We're just going to Lincoln Park."

Fake Shay stuck out her bottom lip. "If you say so, but after this park thing I want to go home and have some fun."

"Oh, don't worry. We'll have a lot of fun soon."

The woman grinned.

Maria's radio crackled to life.

"The park has been cleared of all civilians. A drone shows suspect on the way in a red Ferrari, ETA fifteen minutes."

Maria rose and pushed open the back doors of the van. "Okay, men. I want to make this clear. We're going to try and capture this suspect, but she should be considered armed and extremely dangerous. We have every reason to believe she is an enhanced threat. Officer safety should be prioritized over capture. This suspect has been linked to multiple homicides on the East Coast and is believed to be a professional hitman. Don't expect remorse or restraint. If she so much as blinks at you the wrong way, take her ass down. Am I clear?"

"Yes, Lieutenant," the men shouted in unison.

"What if Brownstone shows up?" Sergeant Weber asked.

"Fuck Brownstone. Same goes for him. If he wants to go down defending some killer, not my fucking problem."

Maria snorted. All it would take was one swing or shot from Brownstone in defense of this NY killer and the lieutenant would have him. The city wouldn't drool over a man who'd hurt cops to protect a killer.

I hope you do show up, Brownstone. That would make my whole fucking decade.

James parked his truck up the street from the park. No

police were in sight, but there was a curious lack of normal cars as well. The authorities had obviously cleared the area.

He hopped out and walked toward Fake Shay as she exited her vehicle.

"Remember this place?" James nodded toward the park.

"Uh, yes?"

"You don't remember our first kiss here?" He forced a fake laugh. "I guess we were both pretty drunk."

The woman chuckled. "I kind of remember, but, yeah you're right."

They walked up the street and the grass and baseball fields of the park came into view. James pointed to a bench about twenty yards away.

"I want you to sit there. I have a very special surprise for you."

"A special surprise?"

James winked. He almost gagged.

"The kind of special surprise that all women expect from their man."

His stomach turned. Why the fuck had he agreed to Peyton's fake proposal plan? For all he knew, the fucker was just doing this to mess with him.

Fake Shay clasped her hands together and smiled, then sashayed toward the bench. "Okay, James. Hurry."

The bounty hunter walked toward his truck. His hands twitched. He wanted to pull out his gun and end this fake bitch himself, but the only way to get AET off Shay's back was to deliver Shay to them, and the fake would have to do.

"Fuck!" Maria gritted her teeth. "Brownstone's leaving."

Sergeant Weber looked her way. "Should we wait?"

"No. We need to take her *now*. All units advance. All units advance."

AET officers burst from bushes, behind cars, and around corners with their weapons raised.

The dark-haired killer leapt up from the bench, her head jerking back and forth.

Maria flipped the safety off on her rifle. "LAPD AET. You are under arrest on suspicion of homicide. You will drop to your knees and place your hands behind your head now."

The woman snorted. "You insects think you have any chance against me?"

Maria offered her own snort. "Bitch, please—just give me a reason. You come along nice and quietly and answer a few questions for us, you might be able to see the outside of a cell before the twenty-second century."

A blade of shadow extended from the suspect's right arm.

"Cease the magic immediately or you will be fired upon!"

"*He* did this, didn't he?" The suspect laughed. "Oh, he's worthy after all. It's too late, though. He can't hide from me; not anymore. I'll show him why he should despair. Prepare to die, insects."

Maria growled. "Light this bitch up!"

24

Blue bolts of electricity along with a hail of bullets flew at the dark-haired killer but didn't pierce the dark, shadowy aura surrounding her. The AET officers kept up their assault, but the bullets disappeared. That was even more unsettling than if they had bounced off.

The suspect whipped out her arm, and a black sphere shot from her hand and slammed into the nearest AET officer.

He grunted and stumbled backward. The anti-magic deflector around his neck, untouched, would have been clear and mostly translucent with a hint of blue. His was a murky brown.

Maria ejected her magazine from her rifle and reloaded. "Get some cover!" She snapped her rifle up and fired a burst as she backed toward the AET van.

The killer rushed toward another man and shoved her shadow blade into his chest. He screamed, and as he fell his deflector turned black and shattered.

"Damn it." Maria gritted her teeth.

Two other officers grabbed the man and pulled him backward.

"Do you see the truth now? You have no chance of beating me, especially with the pathetic tools you've brought." The dark-haired killer chuckled as bullets and stun blasts continued to pound into her. "I'll lower myself to harvest your pathetic life energy. At least in death, you'll serve some use."

The lieutenant seethed at the taunt. In a sense, the suspect was right. They'd underestimated her, and now cops were getting hurt because of it.

Maria jumped into the van. "Blow that bitch away with the rockets!"

A tactical drone emerged from behind a tree and fired a salvo of rockets at the suspect. The flames of the explosions enveloped her. She emerged a few seconds later, blood streamed down her face.

The bitch wasn't indestructible. That was all Maria had needed to know.

"Insects, know your place!"

The woman leapt into the air, dark wings of shadow springing from her back. She charged the drone and sliced it in half with her shadow blade before swooping down and slicing two more emerging from the trees into pieces. So much for the follow-up AET air barrage.

Her wings vanished, and she fell to the ground. On impact, a circular blast of dark energy shot from her, knocking down most of the nearby AET officers.

Several deflectors turned murky or black. Others shattered.

"Fuck." Maria tossed her rifle to the ground and grabbed a long-barreled silver railgun off the wall. The weapon was almost as long as she was tall.

"I was going to let you flee, but now I will make sure that every last one of you dies."

"Damn it." Maria hefted the railgun up and rested it on her armored shoulder. She slid back the charging bolt and the weapon hummed. "Let's see if you can choke this down, bitch." She pulled the trigger.

The round blasted out of the weapon with a roar and slammed into the killer before the lieutenant could even blink. The killer jerked backward and flew through the air before slamming into the ground, rolling, and stopping face down. The shadowy nimbus remained around her body.

Maria lowered the railgun and picked her assault rifle back up. She ejected the magazine and swapped in a clip of anti-magic bullets from the van. Each round cost more than she made in a year, and they weren't even guaranteed to pierce magical defenses.

"Just stay down, bitch."

The dark-haired killer stirred and hopped to her feet, laughing. A huge hole marred her chest. The railgun round had pierced her defenses, but she also was rather inconveniently not dead.

Inky darkness sealed the wound. The hole remained, but it was as if the shadows themselves were becoming one with the body.

Maria sighed. "Well, shit."

"Technology cannot win against magic, insects!" the

woman yelled. She thrust her palms forward and a dark orb about the size of a basketball blasted toward the van.

Maria jumped out of the vehicle just as the orb smashed into it. The back exploded in a blue-green flame, knocking the lieutenant to the ground, and the flames licked at her. She hissed at the pain and fumbled to pull off her helmet and one of her arm guards.

Shit. It's not hot, it's fucking cold. Super-fucking-cold.

The helmet and arm guard hit the ground and shattered like ice. Her deflector was solid black now, all but useless. Her shoulder ached from the cold, the skin tender as if frostbitten.

Freed of the freezing armor pieces, Maria jumped for her rifle.

The killer shot toward another officer in a blur. She slashed him with her shadow blade, and he collapsed with a scream.

Two officers farther out blasted grenades from their undercarriage launchers. The grenades exploded around the woman, and she stumbled to her knees. Blood covered her face now, but she remained smiling.

Maria flipped her rifle to full auto. "Time to piss off some taxpayers." She squeezed and held the trigger. The rifle roared, unleashing the rune-marked bullets in a steady stream toward the suspect.

The dark-haired killer jerked as each bullet ripped into her. The AET lieutenant emptied the magazine.

The suspect collapsed to her knees, her perforated body held together by shadow, but the dark aura surrounding her before had vanished. Maria tossed the rifle to the ground, pulled out a pistol, and advanced.

The dark-haired killer laughed and coughed up blood. "In the end you still needed magic, insects." She lifted a hand and shadows gathered around it. "It won't be enough in the end."

Maria glared at the woman. "I don't care where the tool comes from as long it helps me put down criminals. I'm fucking AET, and I'll always make sure it's enough to stop assholes like you." She shot the woman in the head.

The suspect fell back, blood blossoming from the wound. All the shadows in her wounds fled, leaving her a bullet- and hole-riddled corpse.

"Who the fuck was she?" Maria whispered.

The AET lieutenant took several deep breaths and clutched her arm. "How is everyone?" she asked after a good thirty seconds. She shook her head to refocus herself.

Sergeant Weber staggered toward her, wincing. "Ambulances on are the way, lieutenant. Got several wounded, but no one's dead. I think pretty much everybody lost their deflectors though."

Maria surveyed the groaning and wounded men and women of the AET and curled her hands into fists, pissed at the magic freak who had almost killed the team.

"Good. The whole point of those damned things is to save our lives."

"The captain's going to be upset that we used them all up on one suspect."

The lieutenant snorted. "I emptied a full thirty-round clip of anti-magic bullets into her too. And she blew up one of the vans. And took out all the drones. It wasn't like we could ask her for a budget range before we took her down."

Weber blinked. "Shit. Between all that and the deflectors, that's got to be millions of dollars."

"Imagine if that bitch had decided to open up like that at this park on a Saturday with nothing but civilians around! It would have been a massacre. I don't give a shit how much it costs. When assholes like that pop up, we need to put them down so they know it's not open season on humanity."

Sirens sounded in the distance. The ambulances were closing.

Maria sighed. "Doesn't matter. The bitch is dead now. We just need to get our guys to the hospital." She nodded toward a nearby bench. "Just rest until the ambulance gets here."

She snapped a picture of the corpse with her phone and sent it to Special Agent Danforth's number, then dialed the man. She didn't even let him speak when the call connected. "Tell me that was her."

The agent didn't speak for several seconds. "Son of a bitch, that *was* her. How the fuck did she fake her death before?"

"She was tossing out some high-end magic. I don't know who she was, or even *what* she was. Faking her own death was probably low-end shit for her."

"Damn. Sorry you had to deal with that."

Maria snorted. "Bitch should have stayed on the East Coast."

James frowned at the position of his couch in the still-mostly-empty living room. Not centered enough. He knew what Shay would say about him caring so much, but it was his house, not hers. He would arrange his furniture the way he preferred.

Proper organization from the beginning would make laying everything else out simpler. Even if the rest of his life couldn't be simple anymore, at least his fucking house could.

James grunted. He hadn't thought about what might be best for Alison. He'd need to think a little harder about how to best set up all the furniture, taking her needs into account.

Guess you can't keep things simple when you have a kid, blind or not.

Sergeant Mack knocked on the open door.

James looked up. "Hey, Mack."

"Hey, Brownstone." The cop took a moment to look around. "Glad you're moving back into your own place, even if it means I'm losing a tenant. The new house looks great, though."

"Yeah, they did a good job. Plus, I've got a fresh paint job, unlike my old place."

"When are you going to have everyone over?"

James shrugged. "I'll have some sort of party or shit once everything's ready. We can grill out back."

"I look forward to it. I love a good housewarming." Mack blew out a breath. "I came over to mostly give you a warning. Didn't want to bring down your day, but thought you should know."

"Know what?"

"Something big went down in Lincoln Park yesterday

with AET. Real big. I don't know all the details because they are still keeping a lot of it hush-hush while they investigate the suspect's background." Mack shrugged. "I do know they killed someone serious. From what I've heard, the suspect would have easily been a level-six bounty in terms of power."

James shrugged. "Huh. Didn't hear anything about any level sixes in town. I would have been happy to have helped."

"Yeah, got to have a bounty before a bounty hunter would hear about it." Mack glanced over his shoulder as if expecting a surveillance drone to be hovering right behind him. "You see the thing is, Lieutenant Hall, she's happy. Super-damn happy, and that's creeping me out. Because the only thing that makes her happy lately is doing something to you."

"Like I said, don't know anything about level six bounties."

"You sure this wasn't some sort of Harriken assassin shit? Some left-over guy who wanted his shot at the Scourge of Harriken?"

James grunted. "The Harriken aren't a problem anymore."

The truth was, he had no idea who the woman had been. The only thing he had known was that she was trouble, and his instincts had been proven right, given what Mack was saying.

A residual Harriken assassin, or perhaps some last gasp from the Nuevo Gulf Cartel. It didn't matter now. She was dead.

Mack clapped James on the shoulder. "You're a good man, James Brownstone. Just be careful."

"I'm always careful."

"Raiding buildings filled with Japanese gangsters is careful?"

James shrugged. "That's careful for me."

The cop chuckled, shook his head, and headed for his car.

The real question was if the mysterious highly-powered Fake Shay would be convincing enough for AET.

The real Shay will be pissed if she comes back and has to deal with my AET shit.

James grunted and returned his attention to his couch.

About an hour later, two police cruisers pulled up to the curb. Four uniformed officers stepped out, including Lieutenant Hall. She walked with a slight limp.

James stepped onto his porch. "Nice day, isn't it, Lieutenant?"

She held up a small glass sphere. "Know what this is, Brownstone?"

"An arts and crafts project?"

"Very fucking funny. Nope, it's an Orb of Truth."

James grunted. "I've read about those. Didn't the Supreme Court say they aren't admissible in court?"

Lieutenant Hall sneered. "You'll make a great jailhouse lawyer, Brownstone. That's assuming you survive more than a day in the ultramax once everyone hears you're in there." She held up the orb. "You need to update your law books. They can't be used as the sole evidence for investigation, but if they lead to something else they're totally admissible, asshole."

"I'm guessing you want to ask me some questions, then?"

The cop pulled her phone out and held it up. An image of a bullet-riddled Shay was on the screen.

James' stomach twisted, and bile rose in his throat, but he kept his face impassive. The dress was a giveaway. It wasn't Shay. It was the imposter.

Lieutenant Hall grinned. "First question: do you know the name of this woman?"

"No."

The cop looked at the orb then one of the other officers. "This shit turns red when he lies, right? Clear if he's not?"

They all shrugged.

"Useless." Lieutenant Hall rolled her eyes. "Okay, we'll test this. I'm going to ask you, Brownstone, if you're a police officer. You'll answer yes."

James grunted. "Whatever."

"James Brownstone, are you a police officer?"

"Yes."

The orb glowed red and the AET lieutenant's face darkened.

"Have you ever met the woman in this picture?"

"Yes."

The lieutenant blinked. "You have?" She grinned. "Where did you meet her?"

"Yes. I met her at a bar the other night."

"Bullshit." The cop looked at the now non-glowing orb.

"You met the woman in the picture the other night at a bar?"

"Yep."

Desperation covered Lieutenant Hall's face. "Did this woman help you in a fight at LAX?"

"No."

"Do you have any personal knowledge of the murder victims of this woman?"

"No."

The orb remained stubbornly clear.

The lieutenant took a deep breath. "You met her at a bar and decided to take her on a stroll in Lincoln Park?"

"She was interested in going there, but I don't know what her deal was." He shrugged. "Maybe she was some sort of high-end call girl or something. I got a bad vibe from her, so I left her behind. You telling me this woman had to be brought down by AET?"

"*Yeah*, she had to be taken down by AET. She used magic I've never even *heard* of before. We're just lucky we had brought all our top equipment. If we hadn't been wearing our deflectors most of the team would be dead. As it is, a lot of our guys are in the hospital."

James grunted. "I'm sorry to hear that. I know you don't believe it, but when it comes to AET versus criminals I'm always rooting for the AET."

The orb remained clear.

"You're fucking kidding me." The cop shook the phone in James' face. "You're telling me that you don't know anything about this woman being a hitman in New York? You don't know anything about this woman faking her death? The FBI has her linked to a shit-ton of hits. You're an accessory to murder, Brownstone."

"I don't know anything about that woman and her killing people in New York. Like I told you, I met her in a bar and I didn't trust her."

Lieutenant Hall stared at the orb. "For fuck's sake, come on!" She shook it. "You're telling me you've never done any killing with this woman?"

"I can honestly say, so help me God, I've never done any killing with the woman in that picture."

The cop shook her head. "Whatever. Guess you've got good instincts, Brownstone, and you should get on your knees and thank AET."

"I thank all police officers for their service to the city."

"I'm thinking, Brownstone, that someone hired a premium-grade assassin to finish your ass off. A woman who was already supposed to be dead, so no one even knew to watch for her. You're lucky the AET stopped her. Otherwise, she'd probably be using your skull as a drinking cup now."

James nodded. "It's a good thing you stopped her, then."

Maria spun on her heel. "The important thing is that we got a killer off the street."

"Thank you, Lieutenant."

The cop flipped him off.

James chuckled. "She's been spending too much time around Tyler."

25

James was sitting on the couch listening to a podcast about the history of Texas barbeque when his doorbell rang.

"Probably Hall here to rip my balls off with magic." He rose and peered through the peephole. It wasn't an angry AET lieutenant there for an evening tongue lashing, but a stylish man in a suit.

James opened the door. "Trey. I know it hasn't been that long, but it seems like it's been fucking ages since we last talked."

Trey gave James a fist-bump. "That's because our asses have both been so busy, James, cleaning up the trash and making money for the privilege."

The bounty hunter nodded to the couch. "That's the only place I have to sit in the living room for now. Guess I shouldn't have brought in all my bedroom stuff first. Bringing more shit over tomorrow."

"Why you doing all this by yourself?"

James shrugged. "Didn't want to bother anyone."

Trey snorted. "Come on, James, you got friends. Ask our asses to help you move your shit. That's what friends are for."

The bounty hunter nodded slowly. "Thanks, but I've got it, and I want everything set up a particular way. Don't worry about it."

"Okay, your choice. Just saying."

"Everything going okay with the job? I mean, I've been getting your texts and emails, but I just wanted to make sure there's nothing you needed to tell me about."

The other man laughed and shook his head before taking a seat on the couch. "Shit's going well, you know. Real well. I think I should have started this job a long time ago."

James nodded. "Yeah, you're racking up the bounties. Your reputation's going up, too."

"I know they aren't all fancy King Pyros and shit, but I'm doing my part."

James grunted. "Sometimes some of the most important bounties are lower-level. Assholes like Pyro rob banks and hurt people, but some of these white-collar dicks destroy thousands of people's lives with their crap."

Trey considered that for a moment. "I hadn't thought of it that way."

"How is everyone else doing?"

"You ain't seen Royce do his thing yet, have you?"

"Nope. I've seen Marine drill instructors before, but I haven't watched him train anyone."

"Let me tell you, that guy's the real fucking deal." Trey laughed. "He's gonna put my homies into the ground with the way he's running them down. Glad I never joined the fucking military. If they're all like him, it makes thug life look like bullshit in comparison."

James chuckled. "He's not always gonna be an asshole. He has to break them down to build them up, and all that shit."

"Yeah, I know, I know. That's what I tell the whiners, too."

"Whiners? They having trouble adapting?"

Trey shrugged. "Most of the boys are fine. A few of them still need to get with the program, but they have to accept the truth. Our gangbanging days are done." He sighed. "If we can have good jobs where we're on the right side of the law, why do we even need a gang? So we can steal shit from people? Help run drugs?" He shook his head. "Nah. The Brownstone Agency's reputation and your reputation will help keep our neighborhood safe."

"And they accept that? The whiners?

"I keep telling them we're bounty hunters now, or we're helping a bounty hunter." Trey waved a hand. "Don't worry about it, James. I'll keep everyone in line. We might lose a few, and that's a shame, but some people are just born dumbasses. You know what I'm saying?"

James gave him a shallow nod. There was nothing more he could do. Trey and Royce were better suited than he was to change the gang members into bounty hunters. James could offer them the opportunity, but *they* had to seize it.

Trey gave James a sly look. "Speaking of busy, the word on the street is that you delivered some major pain to the

Nuevo Gulf Cartel. You've basically killed those motherfuckers."

"I took a trip to Mexico. Some shit happened while I was down there, and yeah, it involved a few of their guys."

"Huh. What beef do you have with the cartel? I mean, I know they're sons of bitches, but I haven't heard about them doing anything to you." Trey held up a hand. "Not saying you need a special reason, just the level of beatdown you delivered was a little higher than for just some motherfucker who cut you off in traffic."

James shrugged. "They fucked with someone I care about, so I needed to make them not a problem. They are now not a problem."

He resisted a frown. Shay had gone after the two remaining leaders in Europe. They didn't matter, when he thought about it longer. If they weren't dead already, they soon would be.

Trey snapped his fingers. "Damn. Some bitches never learn the lesson, huh? Everyone's saying the cartel is finished. Other cartels are moving onto their turf already, and it's only been days since you went all Brownstone on them. The Mexican cops and military are suddenly not afraid of them anymore. That's some big-time shit, James—even more than the Harriken." He leaned forward. "They were saying on the news, that shit might help Mexico."

"Maybe. Always other scumbags."

"Yeah, but in the backs of their heads they have to be thinking, 'Fuck? What if James Brownstone comes for *me*?' This is *big*-time."

James shook his head. "I wasn't trying to be big-time, and I had help."

"So you'll get help taking down a cartel, but not fucking moving?"

"Yeah, something like that. I was just trying to help a friend out."

Trey laughed. "That's what I respect about you—it's always about watching out for your homies. That's pure-ass motivation, and I can respect that." Trey grinned. "And keep on doing it, big man." He stood.

"Got to go?"

Trey nodded. "Didn't mean to stop by and run, but I've got a big fish I need to snag tomorrow and I have to run down some contacts so I don't embarrass myself by kicking in the wrong door. You ever do that shit?"

"Mistakes happen. Don't worry about it. You're doing great. I didn't know how this would work, but it's better than I could have ever imagined, and that's because I didn't have to sit there and change your fucking diaper from the beginning. Thanks for not being a stupid piece of shit."

"No, you've got it all wrong." Trey saluted. "Thank you, James. For once, my Nana not only loves me, she's proud of me." He turned and left, closing the door behind him.

James considered what Trey had said. The Harriken were destroyed, and the Nuevo Gulf Cartel were bleeding out. The cynic in him told him that it wouldn't make a difference, that criminals always filled the vacuum, but at the same time, maybe he'd played some small part in helping make the world a less shitty place.

Not trying to do anything but live my life and protect my friends and family. I can't help it if these sonsofbitches keep getting in my way.

Two minutes later the doorbell rang again.

"What, did he forget something?"

James searched around for a rogue wallet or phone before opening the door.

Shay stood there holding a large bag. She stepped into the house, weariness evident on her face.

"Not gonna say anything, Brownstone?"

"Welcome back, and what's the name of your research guy?"

"Why are you asking me that?" She eyed him with suspicion.

"Uh…" James rubbed the back of his neck. He wanted to confirm it was the real Shay, but he also didn't want to let her know that he'd convinced Peyton to hold back information. That might lead to trouble.

Shay smirked. "Don't try and tell me you forgot, Brownstone. You don't forget shit."

James shrugged. "I wanted to check that you are actually you."

"Ah. I was wondering when you'd get around to admitting about that bullshit."

"You knew?"

The tomb raider grinned. "Peyton told me about my little impersonator and the AET taking her down."

"I took care of all that shit for you while you were away. I hope you're not too pissed at him."

"Let's just say that I made it clear that he works for me, not you, and that if there's shit that will affect me I need to know about it."

James grunted. "Sorry."

Shay headed over to the couch and plopped down. She crossed her legs and set the bag down next to her.

"Not a big deal. Besides, you cleaned up the mess before it even affected me. I have to give you credit. Sending an AET team after someone is a little slyer than I'd have pegged you for."

James sat down on the other end of the couch. "You can't solve every problem by punching or shooting it."

Shay shrugged. "Sometimes you need someone else to shoot it."

"Yeah, in this case." James chuckled. "Mack told me she was powerful. She would have been a level six if she had been a bounty."

"That meant she could have given you a run for your money."

James nodded. "Maybe. I didn't think she'd be so tough. I feel kind of shitty about it."

"About what?"

"Cops getting hurt."

Shay sighed. "That's on them. They have procedures and all that shit, and it's not like you haven't done tons for this city—despite some of those same cops trying to take you down. Besides, no one died, so don't beat yourself up over it."

"If you say so."

"Do you have any idea who the woman was?"

James shook his head. "No clue. Probably just another assassin."

Shay peered at James. "Peyton wasn't all that clear how you knew she wasn't me."

"She kept coming on to me, going on about how I was her strong man and everything."

Shay laughed. "Seriously? That bitch should have done more research before she pretended to be me."

"Yeah, she was way too nice to be you."

"Fuck you, Brownstone." The woman rolled her eyes, but her expression remained playful.

They sat there in comfortable quiet for a while before James cleared his throat.

"Did you find the last two cartel leaders?"

"Yeah, I found the last two and handled them." Shay shook her head. "It's kind of weird."

"Weird?"

"You have to understand that I didn't use to worry about shit other than the job. I didn't worry about myself and my life. I didn't really have goals. I just kind of existed."

James nodded. "Can't say I was all that different."

"But now everything's different. Not like I'm gonna go around screaming my name at the top of my lungs, but without the Nuevo Gulf Cartel there's no one from my old life looking to kill me. It makes me think a lot more about my future."

"Does that change anything? About your life, your job, where you want to live?"

Shay shook her head. "Nope. The cartel pushed me over the edge, but I was already teetering. I didn't want to end up bleeding out in my kitchen. You see, a conversation started inside me the day I decided to stop being a killer, but I don't think I finished it until this Europe trip." She took a deep breath. "I've finished that long and hard conversation with myself, and I've realized some shit. Important shit about myself and who I am."

James nodded. "Like what? Did you find out you're an

alien too?"

Shay laughed and batted James in the shoulder. "You wish, Alien Boy. I'm a hundred percent human." She let out a contented sigh. "No, what I realized is that the old person is gone. The killer. Only Shay Carson, tomb raider, remains." Shay winked. "Not that I can't still kick ass when I need to."

"Shit's changed a lot for me, too."

"Yeah, I know." Shay gestured around the room. "You've got a new house and a new daughter. And…" She furrowed her brow. "One question, while I'm thinking about it. You knew that woman wasn't me because I don't try and stick my tongue down your throat? Is that the idea?"

James shook his head. "No. It's not like that. She was trying too hard, and a bunch of little things were off."

"Like what?"

The bounty hunter scratched his nose. "She kept calling me James and not Brownstone."

"You notice that kind of thing?" Shay looked surprised. "Seriously?"

"Yeah, why wouldn't I?"

The woman laughed. "Because you're clueless."

James grunted. "I'm not clueless."

"No, you're definitely fucking clueless about a lot of shit, which is why I was so annoyed with you when we first met, and I've seen you get confused by other shit. I don't know if it's an alien thing or a growing up in orphanage thing or an eating too much barbeque thing, but your mind works in strange ways sometimes."

"Hey, you can never eat too much barbeque. You can eat too much pizza, though."

Shay rolled her eyes. "Yeah, keep telling those lies." She sighed. "The copy did get one thing right. I want to copy something from the copy."

"Huh?"

"James isn't such a bad name, and it sounds weird calling you Brownstone when I live in a brownstone." Shay smiled softly.

The sound of his first name on her lips warmed him more than he expected.

The bounty hunter chuckled. "Your choice, but I don't mind."

Shay rose and sauntered to the front door. She locked it. "Anyone else stopping over tonight?"

"Nope. I think everybody's hit me up for the day." James picked up the bag. "What's in here? 440 nylon, probably holding a few things, but no guns or knives. I haven't heard the clink."

Shay smiled. "Yeah, it's not much. It's a toothbrush and a few other things like that."

"A toothbrush?"

She laughed. "See, you really are clueless. Yeah, a toothbrush for when I stay the night. And just so you know, James, my toothbrush will be on the right."

"Oh. I get it now."

She sashayed over to him with her hands on her hips. "Now, one other thing. I'm tired of waiting." She grabbed the back of his neck. "And it's time to stick my tongue so far down your throat it'll curl your toes."

FINIS

DARK IS HER NATURE

Alison's journey continues in The School Of Necessary Magic. Book one in this new series, *Dark is Her Nature*, and is available exclusively at Amazon.

Order Now at Amazon

AUTHOR NOTES - MICHAEL ANDERLE

JUNE 7, 2018

First, THANK YOU for not only reading this story but reading these *Author Notes*, as well!

This book was a bit difficult to do. Not because the characters are 'finished,' but because we are doing SO MUCH with this small family. Alison now has her own series (*The School of Necessary Magic*), we are revealing how the bounty system came into being twenty years ago (*Justice Served Cold – Rewriting Justice Book 01*), and we are pulling back the covers on what Shay is doing when she is not dealing with James and his coat (*I Fear No Evil series*, about to publish book 3).

Turns out she is hunting treasures. Go figure.

However, there is a wish involved, and I think those that are aware of the wish will be doing what is necessary to acquire it.

Including the Drow.

I don't know if you are familiar with Drow characters,

but I happen to find them fascinating. We finally get to see a Drow in action and frankly?

It can be a little scary.

I believe that the Drow on Oriceran are very haughty, because they are brilliant with magic and are physical badasses. They do have a form of honor, in that they are *very* legalistic. They follow the letter of the laws (that they want to) but are HAPPY to turn it on people. That is why the Widowmaker has a twisted desire to drink the blood of her marks but ONLY if they break their vows.

For me, it brought up an interesting question with police work. There will never be any trace of a body with a kill from the Widowmaker. The absolute best they could hope for would be video proof, and she could not know about the video or she would make it go away.

If she is aware of video, she could use magic to hide what is going on. How would you nail an Oriceran?

I bet you would get an Oriceran detective—sort of how the Oricerans needed a human detective to solve the killing of the Light Elf Prince.

On the personal front, I just got back from three weeks of traveling (Pittsburgh, Boston, New York), meeting dozens of people and reuniting with a couple of dozens I already knew. If someone (other than Future Me) had explained what writing about a woman named Bethany Anne would do for my future and the future of my family?

I think I would have started sooner.

Brownstone's success is a particularly edifying one for me. Given that the idea had germinated for a year, and it being (technically) my second effort to create a new series completely outside *The Kurtherian Gambit,* I was on pins and needles until the reviews spoke.

Well, actually I suppose the *sales* spoke, but the reviews are a good indication of the sales.

As we go into the second arc (books 5-8), I am very pleased to admit that James Brownstone is kicking ass on the charts.

Thanks to you!

Further, Alison's book just went up (and all sorts of mayhem with Amazon's delivery of the pre-orders and early orders ensued, thus screwing up our review average.) For whatever reason, Alison's story has intrigued a LOT of readers. Martha and I are both elated, but frankly a bit surprised.

It's only been forty-eight hours since it started selling, but I'm (crossed fingers) hoping that in two weeks I can still say 'h#ly crap!' about the sales we have yet to understand (they're about fifty percent higher than I would think the book would generate.)

And Amazon has fixed the reviews issue. (Some fans gave the book one-star reviews because they received the wrong book. This wasn't an LMBPN issue, and Amazon is still looking into why it happened).

They should realize I'm going to stay on them for leaving one-star reviews up on the book when it was their mistake that caused the fan frustration.

FAN FUN!

Are you going to be in or around Las Vegas on November 8th, 2018? We are looking to get a few fans (ok, two hundred or more) to come to Sam's Town between 3 – 5 pm for a free time for both Authors and Fans which will include book signings, meet & greet, and interacting together. For those who are already coming, THANK YOU.

You will help us figure out what to do in 2019 for a fan-*freaking*-tabulous time. I will be there, Craig Martelle, Martha Carr and a @#@#%@# load of other authors will be joining us. (There will be over five hundred there earlier in the day, so we hope to have a bunch stick around and party like it's 1999.)

Check with your favorite author and ask ;-)

Join us!

Ad Aeternitatem,

Michael Anderle

PS: HAVE YOU GOT A STORY IN YOU?

If you (our fans) are inspired by our Oriceran universes, you can join the fun! The *Kurtherian Gambit Fans Write for Fans Anthologies* have both gone best-seller, and we now have an Oriceran version in the works. You can find the group at https://www.facebook.com/groups/OriceranFansWrite/, or check in with us at the KGU Fans forum at https://www.facebook.com/groups/TKGFansWrite/.

OTHER REVELATION OF ORICERAN
UNIVERSE BOOKS

The Unbelievable Mr. Brownstone

* Michael Anderle *

Feared by Hell (1) - Rejected by Heaven (2) - Eye For An Eye (3) - Bring the Pain (4) - She Is The Widow Maker (5)

I Fear No Evil

* Martha Carr and Michael Anderle *

Kill the Willing (1) - Bury the Past, But Shoot it First (2)

School of Necessary Magic

* Judith Berens *

Dark Is Her Nature (1)

The Leira Chronicles

* Martha Carr and Michael Anderle *

Waking Magic (1) - Release of Magic (2) - Protection of Magic (3) - Rule of Magic (4) - Dealing in Magic (5) - Theft of Magic (6) - Enemies of Magic (7) - Guardians of Magic (8)

The Soul Stone Mage Series

* Sarah Noffke and Martha Carr *

House of Enchanted (1) - The Dark Forest (2) - Mountain of

Truth (3) - Land of Terran (4) - New Egypt (5) - Lancothy (6) - Virgo (7)

The Kacy Chronicles
* A.L. Knorr and Martha Carr *

Descendant (1) - Ascendant (2) - Combatant (3) - Transcendent (4)

The Midwest Magic Chronicles
* Flint Maxwell and Martha Carr*

The Midwest Witch (1) - The Midwest Wanderer (2) - The Midwest Whisperer (3) - The Midwest War (4)

The Fairhaven Chronicles
* with S.M. Boyce *

Glow (1) - Shimmer (2) - Ember (3) - Nightfall (4)

BOOKS BY MICHAEL ANDERLE

For a complete list of books by Michael Anderle, please visit

www.lmbpn.com/ma-books/

All LMBPN Audiobooks are Available at Audible.com and iTunes. For a complete list of audiobooks visit:

www.lmbpn.com/audible

CONNECT WITH MICHAEL ANDERLE

Michael Anderle Social
Website:
http://kurtherianbooks.com/

Email List:
http://kurtherianbooks.com/email-list/

Facebook Here:
https://www.facebook.com/OriceranUniverse/
https://www.facebook.com/TheKurtherianGambitBooks/

Made in the USA
Middletown, DE
18 January 2019